JAPANESE
SHORT STORIES

Ryunosuke Akutagawa

JAPANESE SHORT STORIES

Tuttle Publishing

Published by Tuttle Publishing by special arrangement
with Liveright Publishing Corporation, New York

ISBN 4-8053-0464-2

First Tuttle edition, 1981
Fifth printing, 2000

Printed in Singapore

PREFACE

THE TEN STORIES in this collection were selected with the aim of presenting Akutagawa's finest and most representative writings.

I wish to express my sincere thanks to the following persons for their kind assistance and many valuable suggestions and criticisms; John and Rosaleen McVittie, professors of Meiji University, Tokyo, who read the whole of the manuscript, Mr. C. G. Wells formerly of the Far East Network, Prof. Benjamin F. Sisk of Meiji University, Prof. Theodore J. Kitchen of Aoyama Gakuin University, Mr. Eric Mizuno who all read sections of the manuscript, and to Prof. John McVittie for his excellent introduction.

I especially express my sincere thanks to Mr. Arthur Pell, Editor of Liveright Publishing Corporation, for his valuable suggestions, advice and assistance.

TAKASHI KOJIMA

Tokyo, Japan
August, 1961.

CONTENTS

[7]

ILLUSTRATIONS

JAPANESE SHORT STORIES

INTRODUCTION
A Sprig of Cherry

A SPRIG OF CHERRY

—an Introduction to This Book

WHY ARE YOU reading this book? Perhaps though in search of inspiration or romance you are not quite certain of what to expect. On the other hand, from most English books we know too well what to expect.

Even on television, when we see a "western"—to smell the smoke of burning grass, when we watch a ship tossed on the ocean—to feel the cold sea-spray on our faces, to gall at the sight of raw wounds and to feel the keen edge of the swords in an ancient battle,—ability to experience such thrills of romance is benumbed by the opiate of modern life's many comforts, and rarely extends to entertainment that is radically different and inspiring.

Yet, every day, writers and publishers, fashion designers, producers, artists, do arrive in Far Eastern cities searching for the exotic,—old themes in new make-up. In coming to the East they too are searching for "inspiration," for atmosphere"; without knowing what to expect they are conscious

[13]

of the cliché that "the East is mysterious." If they remain long enough to solve the mystery, they discover that what they want is in the very succinctness of Japanese art; they find that art is not in what is spoken, what is written, but rather in what is implied. It could be said that a blank piece of paper,—ivory white,—is a perfect picture of purity. This might well amuse us until we consider that in the field of sensory perception "pure whiteness" can never exist; it can exist only in aspiration.

The doctrine of *sokuten kyoshi*—self-detachment in pursuit of heaven—was taught by the famous writer, Natsumé Soseki, to his students at the Imperial University of Tokyo in the early years of the Taisho era (in the years of World War I). Happiness exists only in contemplation and imagination, suggested Soseki,—a contention which fascinated his brilliant and extremely sensitive young student, Akutagawa Ryunosuké, who had already admired the detachment evident to some degree in the styles of Prosper Merimée and Anatole France.[1]

Already, through translation and motion pic-

[1] Sometimes his work reminds me of Chatterton, sometimes of Byron, and sometimes of Keats, but it would be tempting sophistry to draw any conclusions from this. His principal interest was English Literature; his graduation thesis was on William Morris. Nevertheless, it seems he was influenced by Mori Ogai who was a keen German Literature scholar. To confound the critic we add that Akutagawa read extensively from Chinese classics.

ture, has Akutagawa been introduced to the West. Already English-language translations of such masterpieces as "Rashomon" and "Kappa" have provided Western readers with an insight into Akutagawa's variation on Soseki's theme,[2]—his pursuit of contentment through self-detachment; and Western readers,—even as the Japanese,—have been fascinated by his polished style and daring revival of old names and legends. Because of his extensive general knowledge and his sharp perception, his self-detachment in the execution of his works, his youthful spirit, and his inclination for long hours of uninterrupted work, without exception his literary creations are all masterpieces,— individualistic in spite of their borrowed themes, saved from being pretentious by their air of historical authenticity; their author gradually succeeded in eliminating all that was not vital to the structure and atmosphere of the story.

Japanese arts, philosophies, religions, literary schools, like any in the world have their variations and innuendoes, but when they choose to be Oriental and do not endeavor to be mere copies of their Occidental counterparts irrespective of the numerous forms, simple or complex, in which they appear, they have a characteristic evanescence; to appreciate art in spite of its adornment, for re-

[2] Many of Soseki's works are available in translation.

ligion to be experienced in spite of the distracting influence of moving hymns and solemn stained glass windows, there must be an instinctive understanding rather than an appreciating by the senses. Consequently, if such be the inspiration to which our minds become conditioned we will, indeed, in our experiencing of art or literature, "smell the burning leaves," and cower before the "keen edged swords"; in Akutagawa's stories we may, if we will, smell the scent of plum blossoms in painted moonlight, hear the courtier painted on the screen playing his plaintive flute.

In contrast with such romance, rare in our time, we find that civilization in the modern world—East and West—demands a devotion to material things. Capital, labor, and science, emerging from a world war have achieved, in part, the outward show of the warriors' dreams of a "new order." Improvements in living standards have brought within the reach of most people such advantages as air conditioners, radio and television, and innumerable other devices to divert the mind in leisure hours. In such an age, reading cannot be the most popular means of escape from irksome routine; and the reading public could hardly find much relaxation in reading matter that dutifully reproduces the atmosphere of the age. Occasionally a publisher or producer is rewarded because he has the courage to present to the public some work which is *new* because it has a spirit of its own; he does not rely on the fashionable current of thought which, being largely utilitarian can *instruct,* but, like "The *Romance* of Nuclear Physics," can hardly entertain.

When Akutagawa's first work appeared it was still the experimental period of Modern Japanese Literature when writers—earnestly wanting to break away from the old traditions that lingered on well after the Restoration of 1868—were still ready to attempt anything new. The magazine to which Akutagawa contributed when he was still an undergraduate was *Shin Shichō* (New Thought); in this periodical Akutagawa's works appeared from 1914 onwards alongside the names of other pioneers such as Kikuchi Kan, Kumé Masao, and Yamamoto Yuzo. In 1915 *Rashomon* (Rashō Gate) first appeared; in 1916 *Hana* (The Nose) was published. In 1918 Akutagawa married,—there being no especial significance in the fact that soon after this event he wrote his famous *Jigoku hen* (Hell's Cataclysm) (translated in this book under the title of "Hell Screen") and *Hokyonin no Shi* (Death of a Christian).

Like the plan of Horikawa Palace itself, the boldness and grandeur of the design of "Hell Screen" are beyond conception. Of tales of horror there are many in the lore of all nations, but it is rare in any language to find in the same story such qualities as horror and elegance, the grotesque presented with a restraint that justifies the most horrible turn-of-events as the most natural fulfillment of destiny. Japanese, unlike English, being a language of understatement, is a most suitable medium for presentation of the macabre atmosphere of "Hell Screen" and only because the plot in its structure too retains the story's unique minor key, can we convey into English the peculiar spirit that pervades "Hell Screen." It is this spirit—this ghost of the Middle Ages that becomes our companion in reading "Hell Screen," as in reading many of the author's other stories; while we read, the medieval ghost looks over our shoulder and reads for us between the lines; it derides the orthodoxy of our Occidental minds, our unromantic comfort in the *rule of law*—that opiate which has dulled in us the sensitivity required to comprehend medieval superstition that pervaded feudal society throughout the ages of the *rule of might;* the death throes of such a society being within the living memory of some Japanese, and because its spirit was powerful enough, imaginative enough, to wage war against democracy in recent years, the Japanese understand instinctively the medieval soul through the experience of it has long since been lost to Western peoples; our historical books and films—in contrast with their Japanese counterparts—reveal that we have not even a superficial awareness of it. There would seem to be little difference between being.

bewitched in the dark ages by a fox, and in modern times being bewitched by an insurance representative; there is some claim to superiority by our ancient forefathers in that they alone were *aware of* their bewitchment; the author of "Hell Screen" is one of the few in our own age who shares with them such superiority.

But Akutagawa was not always pre-occupied in re-creating the macabre. When the night herons flying about under the stars seemed ominous, then indeed they were ominous; if, on the other hand, environment happened to suggest a happier turn-of-events, then they might even have seemed comical. In reading *"Nezumikozō Jirokichi"* we are amused by the idea of a crow's throat being so sore from frosty weather that he is unable to caw. Both plot and style of "Nezumi Kozo" are in a lighter vein, the leisurely story beginning in a leisurely way, "the smoke of glowing tobacco curling lazily in the dying light of the setting sun." Throughout the story there is the atmosphere of the *uki-yoe*, the floating world wood block prints made famous by Hiroshigé and his ilk; in such prints there are many travellers, wearing the same shoes, hat, kimono, brown oil-paper raincoat, and straw sandals; and sometimes even today on Japan's country roads such travellers come to life. Like most travellers he is happy to be on his way, he is sad to be leaving the city, he is glad of a companion to help him beguile the journey; as a man of experience he has developed an astute sense of justice as ironically revealed in the denouement; this flourish of irony would well have satisfied the cyncism that sometimes prevailed in Akutagawa's moods. Akutagawa's photographs, in which keen eyes, high broad cheekbones, and sensitive lips predominate, testify to the truth of the assurance by his literary colleagues that his moods—like his numerous stories —were many and often paradoxical, ranging from periods of brilliant wit to nervous dilemma.

In view of this it is reasonable to assume that in writing *"Hana"* (The Nose) he would have felt keen sympathy with Zenchi whose huge nose, like Cyrano de Bergerac's, was "a national monument." The Japanese are as capable as any people of laughing at human deformity, or of not seeing it at all; in *Hana,* however, the hero's associates, feeling rather sympathy with, and certainly no envy for, the unfortunate man, Zenchi had "risen to hold the respectable post of Chaplain to the Palace Chapel." "What would happen," wondered Akutagawa, "if such a man were to become normal in appearance?"—and in *Hana* attempts to answer this question,—modern theories of human behavior assisting in the interpretation of his 11th century characters. It is difficult to believe that when the story ends we are quite happy about "the long nose dangling in the chill autumn wind of early morning."

A story even more delicate is *"Kumo no Ito"* (The Spider's Thread) in which, with Buddha in Paradise, we are led to stroll along the rim of the lotus pond. Whereupon, the compassionate Buddha, pausing on the fringe of the pond, happens to peep down through the lotus leaves on the surface to where deep below is the abyss of hell. From that point onwards the story could be a Christian parable. There is nothing especially Japanese in the development of "The Spider's Thread" except for the acknowledgment of the harmony between Nature and Gautama Buddha (which, after all, is also a commonly accepted belief elsewhere among Buddhists), and the gentle anticlimax,—the human touch at the end appealing to Japanese naïveté: "In Paradise it is surely getting on for noon."

In such stories, consistent with the pursuit of contentment through self-detachment, Akutagawa indicates that man's own will triumphs over destiny to determine the degree of a man's happiness, a doctrine that was bitterly criticized by many of his contemporary writers who, attempting to advance the struggle for "workers' rights," contended that the proletariat was subject to "the whims of social injustice." Akutagawa's evident disapproval of workers' union-conspiracy was apparent from his ignoring of it, as he was free in conscience to do if he wished; but he naturally stirred the wrath of the militant social writers when his bewitching style revived the romance of the feudal institutions which they despised.

The literary figures of the Meiji era had liked to believe that Japan had completely replaced feudalism with something entirely new; but because they were confused by the precise nature of their new ethics, following spasmodically a variety of Western theologians and philosophers, they were left bewildered by the death of the Meiji Emperor— the patron of their "enlightenment." The real confusion among the Japanese intelligentsia was caused by the suicide of General Nogi, Japan's most illustrious General, who sacrificed his life to follow his Imperial Master across the borders of Death; General Nogi's action was in accordance with the highest precepts of *bushi*—the feudal chivalry which, being immutable and devoid of any complexity, mellowed over many centuries by the dictates of necessity, the Japanese well understood; these precepts were compatible with the Japanese temperament, a clear criterion of conduct, while the imported ideals were often contradictory. The *Shin Richi Ha* (Neo-Intellectual School), of which Akutagawa became a leader, rejected the wholesale importation of foreign ethics, and distrusted bushido because of its lack of adaptability and because it had been used as an excuse for all manner of cruelties. Apparently spurred on by Soseki's [3] research into the intellectualism of 18th century England, the Neo-Intellectuals set about providing some solution to the problem of suggesting an ethical system worthy of Japanese life and consistent with the age. Akutagawa sought the solution in attaining self-detachment through his art, a simple solution that did not satisfy his author associates.

This ethical dilemma is evident in the story entitled *"Otomi no Teiso"* (Otomi's Virginity). It is a story of pride in chivalry and the preservation of personal dignity and honor. There is some inspiration felt in the act of a person of humble origin who, presumably lacking in moral training, is faced with the choice of safeguarding the honor and dignity of her mistress or of maintaining her own; she loves her mistress, and she loves "Pussy"; instinctively she decides what to do according to the situation in which she is placed; and instinct proves a wise judge. The story is a masterpiece in the study of individualism, a monument to Oriental evanescence. Naturalists would clamor for the fulfillment of desire, but the reader of this story, like Otomi as Shinko's carriage passes by, feels relieved of care,—a moment of self-detachment.

[3] Natsumé Soseki: "Bungaku Hyoron" Meiji 1942.

Akutagawa's outlook, however, is not as egotistic as Japanese literary critics like to quote one another in contending. "The Tangerines," (*Mikan*, in Japanese) is one of the many stories that indicates he was willing to admit the influence of others' actions in assisting, unconsciously, the individual in achieving some measure of detachment. The country girl who is the heroine of "The Tangerines" was a symbol of "vulgar realities in human shape ... the symbol of an unintelligible and wearisome life ... but within a few minutes I felt life welling up within me ... I completely forgot I was bored, I became oblivious to the apparent absurdity of my meaningless life." "The Tangerines" reminds me of the *haiku* poetry of Japan [4]— the few brief syllables of poetry in which the Japanese, with skill varying according to intensity of feeling, are inclined to enshrine the ecstasy of the moment, the succinctness of Zen.

Yado no haru nanimo naki koso nanimo are

(SODŌ)

Springtime,
and in my hut
—nothing:
Yet everything!

"*Yonosuke no Hanashi*" (The Story of Yonosuke) embodies this "touch on life," and has a

---

[4] Akutagawa himself wrote some *haiku*.

theme as old as human life, a theme which is epitomized in one of the briefest but most dynamic words in the English language,—"sex." This story serves to illustrate Akutagawa's position that the ecstasy is in the expectation, not in the fulfillment. In ancient Rome it was said that the anti-climax upon fulfillment is the annihilation of the thrill of nature's inducement. "My story begins at the moment my knee touched hers . . . Was she feeling as I felt? . . . I enjoyed her clear eyes . . . I enjoyed the delicate shades of her eyelashes slightly moving on her fresh cheeks. I enjoyed the charm of her fingers flexing on her lap . . . The rest I leave to imagination." This is where Akutagawa's story ends, and where the reader's really begins; it begins with what is unspoken, with what is unwritten; it is the delicate realm of self-detachment.

Akutagawa mentions in his reminiscences that he tried to find in historical data an escape from the gloom of his love-affairs, and, having escaped from the snares of desire, to attain to enlightenment. "I simply wanted to write novels divorced from reality," he wrote in *Ano koro no Jibun no koto* (My own affairs at the time). As he did in the "Story of Yonosuke," he succeeded in this through the medium of his art, and with the minimum subjective intrusion was able to peer at the intricacies of human aspiration. Since he was born in Tokyo and lived there all his life except for a brief tour of China, and had absorbed much of the Bohemianism of the writers' circle, we may say that his objective approach easily extended itself to *"Ikkai no Tsuchi"* (A Clod of Soil, 1924) in which, as its title implies, we are introduced to some simple country folk. This too is reminiscent of the *haiku*. Hiroji, the little boy, is content to amuse himself with a sprig of cherry blossom,—not to be interpreted only as a sign of his lack of play-things, but as typical of some intangible quality of Japanese life.[5] Moreover, grandmother Osumi's smoking of cigarette butts is no confession of extreme poverty; "she had carefully collected the cigarette butts left by her (dead) son"; it is an innate habit among the lowly classes of Japan— even in this period of national prosperity, to use and re-use to exhaustion everything usable; it would not be an over-statement to interpret this habit as an unconscious virtue in the Buddhist pilgrimage towards zero. Hiroji's mother died, and the grandmother, Osumi, lay awake thinking that her daughter-in-law's death "had brought her great happiness . . . Her memory vividly recalled a certain night nine years before; on that night she had sighed in the same way; that had been the night

[5] I have seen my own five-year-old son, Julian,—brought up in Tokyo among Japanese friends and so by nature quite Japanese,—prefer to designate a mere stone a boat than to play with the several toy boats in his toy-chest.

after the funeral of her only son ... She heard the clock strike four; the sleep of the weary fell upon her. At the same time the sky over the thatched roof was bathed in the first chill grey streaks of dawn from the eastern horizon." Osumi's attitude is puzzling to the Western mind, but Akutagawa understood it, not as the callousness which Western ideals must assume it to be, but as the Oriental relief experienced upon the elimination of some of life's problems in the vacuum of nothingness.

If we realize this, then we can comprehend why at the early age of thirty-five years, Akutagawa chose to enjoy that experience himself. He had gone as far as he could in his pursuit of self-detachment through creation of literary works; the only step forward was in the direction of death through self-annihilation. When he took this step, the public widely grieved, and his fellow writers—the leader among whom was the illustrious Kikuchi Kan, wept bitterly with Akutagawa's wife and three boys; and yet because they were Japanese, they understood.

In the translation of these stories, Akutagawa's fine phrases have been rendered faithfully into English. In a few instances, the translator (being Japanese) has used several familiar expressions to emphasize the graphic. But what we might feel we lose from the fact that the English is not the translator's natural tongue, is offset by our own awareness that the translator's thoughts, his feelings, his character, are—as were Akutagawa's—*Japanese*.

Then, in your search of inspiration in this book, you should know what you might expect.

In the West you say: My cup is half-full, let's fill it; in the East we say: the cup is half-empty, let's empty it.

JOHN McVITTIE

University of Tokyo
August, 1961

THE HELL SCREEN

I

THE GRAND LORD of Horikawa is the greatest lord that Japan ever had. Her later generations will never see such a great lord again. Rumor has it that before his birth, Daitoku-Myo-O [1] appeared to her ladyship, his mother, in a dream. From birth he was a most extraordinary man. Everything he did was beyond ordinary expectations. To mention just a few examples, the grandeur and bold design of his mansion at Horikawa are far beyond our mediocre conceptions. Some say that his character and conduct parallel those of the Emperor I [2] of China and the Emperor Yang.[3] But this comparison may well be likened to the blind man's description of the elephant. For it was far from his intention

---

[1] Daitoku-Myo-O * is a three-faced and six-armed god that guards the west, astride a large white bull, being one of the five great kings that appear in the Chanavyua sutra.

[2] The First Emperor of China established the great Chinese Empire in 221 B.C.

[3] The Chinese Emperor Yang established the Sui Dynasty in 604 A.D.

to enjoy a monopoly of all glory and luxury. He was a man of great stature who would rather share pleasures with all the people under his rule.

Only so great a ruler could have been able to pass unhurt through the gruesome scene of the veritable pandemonium enacted in front of the imperial palace. Moreover, it was undoubtedly his authoritative command that exorcised the nightly hauntings of the spirit of the late Minister of the Left [4] from his mansion, the gardens of which were a famed imitation of the picturesque scenery of Shiogama.[5] Horikawa had such great influence that all the people of Kyoto, young and old, respected him as highly as if he were a Buddha incarnate.

Once on his way home from a plum-blossom exhibit at the Imperial court, one of the bulls pulling his cart broke away and injured an old man who happened to be passing by. It is rumored that even in such an accident the old man, clasping his hands together in reverence, expressed his gratitude for having been knocked over by the Grand Lord's bull.

Thus his life was full of memorable anecdotes which might well be handed down to posterity.

[4] "The Minister of the Left" was, next to the Premier, the highest Minister of State along with the Minister of the Right.
[5] "Shiogama" is a picturesque fishing village in the north-east of Japan.

At a certain Imperial banquet he made a gift of thirty white horses. Once when the construction work of the main bridge was snagged, he made a human pillar of his favorite boy attendant to propitiate the wrath of the god. Years ago he had a Chinese priest, who had introduced the medical art of a celebrated Chinese physician, lance a carbuncle on his hip. It is impossible to enumerate all such anecdotes. But of all these anecdotes, none inspires one with such overpowering horror as the history of the hell screen which is now among the Lord's family treasures. Even the Grand Lord, whose presence of mind had never been shaken, seemed to have been extraordinarily shocked. Furthermore, his attendants were all frightened out of their wits. Having served him for more than twenty years, I had never witnessed such a terrifying spectacle.

But before telling you the story, I have to tell you about Yoshihide who made a ghostly painting of Hell on the screen.

II

Now as for Yoshihide, some people still remember him. He was such a celebrated master of painting that no contemporary could equal him. When, what I am going to relate happened, he must have been well past his fiftieth year. He was stunted in growth, and was a sinister-looking old man, all skin and bones. When he came to the Grand Lord's mansion, he would often wear a clove-dyed hunting suit and soft head-gear. He was extremely mean in nature, and his noticeably red lips, unusually youthful for his age, reminded one of an uncanny animal-like mind. Some said, that he had got his red lips because of his habit of licking his paintbrush; although I doubt if this were true. Some slanderous people said that he was like a monkey in appearance and behavior, and nicknamed him *"Saruhide"* (monkey hide).

This Saruhide had an only daughter, who was fifteen years old, and was serving as a lady's maid at the Grand Lord's mansion. Quite unlike her father, she was a charming girl and of extraordinary beauty. Having lost her mother in her very early years, she was precocious, and moreover, intelligent and observant beyond her age. Thus she won the good graces of her ladyship, and was a favorite with the attendants.

About that time, a tame monkey was presented to the Lord from the Province of Tanba, west of Tokyo. The Lord's young son, who was at his most mischievous age, nicknamed the animal "Yoshihide."

This name so much the more added to the ridiculousness of the funny animal that everyone in the mansion laughed at him. If that had been all, all would have fared well with him. But as it was, whenever the monkey climbed up the pine-tree in the garden or soiled the mat of the Little Lord's room, indeed, whatever it did, they shouted his name and teased him.

One day Yoshihide's daughter, Yuzuki, was passing along the long corridor, carrying in her hand a spray of pink winter plum blossoms, with a note attached to it, when she saw the monkey running toward her from beyond the sliding door. He seemed injured and had no desire to climb up the pillar with his usual agility. In all likelihood he had sprained one of his legs. Then whom should she see, but the Little Lord running after him swinging a switch in his hand, shouting, "Stop tangerine thief! Stop! Stop!" At the sight of this, she hesitated a moment. Just then the monkey, came running over, and giving a cry, clung to the bottom of her skirt. Suddenly, she could no longer find it in her heart to restrain her pity. Holding the spray of plum-blossom in one hand, she swung open the sleeve of her mauve-colored robe with the other, and gently took up the monkey.

"I beg your pardon, my lord," she said, in a sweet voice, making a respectful bow before the Little Lord. "He is only a beast, please pardon him, my lord."

"Why do you protect him?" Looking displeased,

[33]

the Little Lord stamped his feet two or three times. "The monkey is a tangerine thief, I tell you."

"He is only a beast, my lord," she repeated.

Then with an innocent but sad smile, she made so bold as to say, "To hear the word Yoshihide rebuked, I am quite upset, as if my father were chastised." At this remark, naughty child that he was, he gave in.

"I see," the Little Lord said reluctantly. "Since you plead for your father's sake, I'll give him a special pardon."

Then throwing away his switch, he turned and went back toward the sliding door through which he had come.

III

From that time on the girl and the monkey became very good friends. She tied a beautiful crimson ribbon around the animal's neck, and also hung from it a little gold bell which the princess had given her. The animal on his part would on no account leave her presence. Once when the girl was laid up with a slight cold, the little monkey sat at her bedside, and with apparent concern, he watched over her, gnawing on his nails.

After this time, strange as it might sound, no one would tease the little monkey as they used to. On the contrary, they all took to petting him. At last even the Little Lord himself came to toss him a persimmon or a chestnut. Once when he caught a knight in the very act of kicking the animal, he is said to have been extremely incensed. This news reaching his ears, the Lord is said to have given gracious orders that the girl should be brought before his presence with the little monkey in her arms. With reference to this incident, he must also have heard how it was that she had come to make a pet of the animal.

"You are a good and dutiful daughter. I am well pleased with your conduct," the Lord said, and presented her with a scarlet robe as a reward. The monkey, mimicking her deferential obeisance in expressing her gratitude, raised the robe to his forehead, to the immense amusement and pleasure of the Lord. It should be recalled that the Lord took the girl into his good graces because he had been impressed with her filial piety which led her to make a pet of the monkey, and not because he was an admirer of the charms of the gentle sex, as rumor had it. There were some justifiable grounds for the rumor, but about these subjects I may have the opportunity of talking further later when I find more time. Now let me limit my description to saying that the Lord was not a personage to fall in love with such a lowly girl as a painter's daughter, no matter how charming she was.

Highly honored, the girl withdrew from the

Lord's presence. Being a naturally wise and intelligent girl, she did nothing to incur the jealousy of her gossipy fellow maids. On the contrary, this honor won their favor and popularity for both herself and the monkey. She was, above all, received into such particular favor by the princess that she was hardly ever found away from the latter's presence and she never failed to share the latter's company in her excursion carriage.

Now setting aside the girl for the time being, let me tell you about her father, Yoshihide. Although the monkey, Yoshihide, came to be loved by everyone, the painter, Yoshihide, was as much hated by everyone as before, and continued to be called "Saruhide" behind his back.

The Abbot of Yokawa hated Yoshihide as if he were a devil. At the mere mention of his name, he would turn black with anger and abhorrence. Some say that this was because Yoshihide painted a caricature depicting the Abbot's conduct. However, this was a mere rumor current among the common people and may have had no foundation in fact. Anyhow, he was unpopular with everybody who knew him. If there were any who did not speak ill of him, they were only two or three of his fellow painters or those who knew his paintings but knew nothing of his character.

Really he was not only mean to look at, but he had such shocking habits that they made him a repellent nuisance to all people. For this he had no one but himself to blame.

IV

Now let me mention his objectionable habits. He was stingy, harsh, shameless, lazy, and avaricious. And worst of all, he was so haughty and arrogant that "his being the greatest painter in the whole of Japan" was hanging from the tip of his nose. If his arrogance had been limited to painting, he would not have been so objectionable. Moreover, he was so conceited that he had a profound contempt for all customs and practices in life.

Here is an episode about him told by a man who had been under his apprenticeship for many years. One day a famous medium in the mansion of a certain lord fell into a trance under the curse of a spirit, and she delivered a horrible oracle. Turning a deaf ear to the oracle, he made a careful sketch of her ghastly face with brush and ink which he found at hand. In his eyes, the curse by an evil spirit may have been nothing more than a jack-in-the-box for children.

This being his nature, he would in picturing a heavenly maiden, paint the face of a harlot, and in picturing the god of fire, the figure of a villain. He committed many such sacrilegious acts. When he was brought to task, he declared with provoking indifference, "It's ridiculous for you to say that the gods and Buddhas I have painted should ever be able to punish their painter." This so amazed all his apprentices that many of them took leave of him immediately in fearful anticipation of terrible consequences. After all, he was arrogance incarnate who thought himself the greatest man under the sun.

Accordingly, one can understand how highly he esteemed himself as a painter. However, his brushwork and colorings were so completely different from those of other painters that many of his contemporaries who were on bad terms with him, would speak of him as a charlatan. They claimed that famous paintings by "Kawanari," [6] "Kanaoka," [6] and other master artists of the past have graceful episodes attached to them. Rumor has it that you can almost smell the delicate fragrance of the plum blossoms on moonlight nights and almost hear the courtier on the screen playing his flute. But all paintings by Yoshihide have the reputation of being unpleasant and uncanny. For example, take his painting representing the five phases of the transmigration of souls which he had painted on the gate of the Ryugai Temple. If you pass from under the gate late at night, you can almost hear

[6] Both "Kawanari" and "Kanaoka" are celebrated Japanese painters of the tenth century.

the sighing and sobbing of the celestial maidens. Some say they even smelled the offensive odor of the rotting bodies. The Grand Lord's court ladies, whose likenesses Yoshihide painted at the Lord's command, all fell ill as if their souls had left them and died within three years. Those who disparage his paintings say that all this is because they are works of his black art.

Yet, as I told you, he was an extremely cross-grained crank, and was boastful of his very perversity. Once when the Grand Lord said to him, "You seem to have a strong partiality for the ugly," he replied, with a grin on his red lips, "Yes, my Lord, unaccomplished artists can't perceive beauty in the ugly." Admitting that he was the greatest painter in the whole country, how could he ever have been so presumptuous as to make such a haughty remark in the presence of the Grand Lord. His apprentices secretly nicknamed him "Chira-Eiju" to slander his arrogance. "Chira-Eiju" is, I presume you know, a vainglorious long-nosed goblin that flew over to Japan in olden times.

However, Yoshihide, who was a perverse scoundrel beyond description, had one tender side showing that he was not altogether lacking in human kindness.

V

He loved his only daughter, who was a Lady-in-Waiting, with a love bordering on madness. She was a girl of very sweet disposition, and devoted to her father. On the part of Yoshihide, incredible as it may sound, he doted on his daughter to the point of infatuation, and would lavish money upon her kimono, hairpins, and whatnots for her adornment, although he never contributed his tithes or mites to any Buddhist temple.

But all his love for his daughter was blind, and wild. He never gave a thought to finding her a good husband. On the contrary, if anyone had attempted to make any advances to her, he would have had no scruples in hiring street rascals to waylay him. Even when she was summoned to be a chambermaid at the gracious command of the Grand Lord, he was so displeased that he looked as sour as vinegar even when he was brought before the very presence of the Grand Lord. The rumor that the Grand Lord, enamored of the girl's beauty, summoned her to his service in the face of her father's strong disapproval, may probably have originated in the imagination of those who were acquainted with such circumstances.

Rumor aside, so much is certain that Yoshihide, out of his indulgent love for his daughter, had an irresistible desire that she should be released from her service. Once when at the Grand Lord's command he painted a picture of a cherub, he accomplished a masterpiece by making a life-sketch of the latter's favorite page.

Highly gratified, the Grand Lord said to the painter, "Yoshihide, I am pleased to grant any request of yours."

"If it pleases your lordship," Yoshihide was audacious enough to say, "Allow me to request that my daughter be released from your service."

Apart from other households, whoever else in the world could ever have made such a presumptuous request of the Grand Lord of Horikawa with regard to the favorite lady-in-waiting, no matter how dearly he may have loved her? With an air of some displeasure, the magnanimous Grand Lord remained silent for a while, staring Yoshihide hard in the face.

"No, I can't grant that," he spat out, and left abruptly. There may have been some four or five such occasions. Now it seemed to me that each time his Lordship looked at Yoshihide with less favor and with growing coldness in his eyes. This must have caused his daughter to worry over her father. When she retired to her room, she was often found sobbing, biting the sleeve of her kimono. Thereafter rumor spread all the more that the Grand Lord was enamored of the girl. Some say that the whole history of the hell-screen may be traced to her refusal to comply with the Grand Lord's wishes. However, I do not believe that this could have been true.

It seems in our eyes that his Lordship did not allow the girl to be dismissed from his service, because he took pity on her family circumstances and had graciously considered to keep her in his mansion and let her live in ease and comfort rather than to send her back to her cross, obstinate father. Undoubtedly he had made a "favorite" of such a charming sweet-tempered girl. However, it is a far-fetched distortion of fact to attribute all this to the amorous motives of his Lordship. No, I dare say that it is an entirely unfounded lie.

Be that as it may, it was at the time when his Lordship had come to look upon Yoshihide with considerable disfavor that he summoned him to his mansion and commanded him to paint on a screen a picture of Hell.

VI

The hell screen was a consummate work of art, presenting before our eyes the vivid and graphic portrayal of the terrible scenes of Hell.

First of all in its design, his painting of Hell was quite different from those of other artists. In a corner of the first leaf of the screen on a reduced scale were painted the ten Kings of Hell and their households while all the rest consisted of terrible flames of fire roaring and eddying around and around the Mountain of Swords and the Forest of Lances, which, too, seemed ready to blaze up and melt away into flames. Accordingly, except for the yellow and blue patches of the Chinese-designed costume of the infernal officials, wherever one might look, all was in blazing flames, black smoke swirling around and sparks shooting up like burning gold dust fanned in a holocaust of fire.

This brushwork alone was sufficient to startle the human eye. The criminals writhing in agony amidst the consuming Hell fire were not like those represented in ordinary pictures of Hell. For here in the portrayal of sinners was set forth, a whole array of people in all walks of life from nobles and dignitaries to beggars and outcasts; courtiers in dignified court dress, coquettish wives of knights in elaborate costumes, priests praying over the rosaries hanging from their necks, samurai students on high wooden clogs, girls in gaudy gala dress, fortune-tellers clad in the robes of Shinto priests—there were an endless number of them. Therein people of all descriptions, tortured by bull-headed hellbounds amidst blazing flames and raging smoke, were fleeing in all directions like so many autumn leaves scattered by a blast of wind. There were women apparently looking like shrine mediums, with their hair caught in forks and their limbs drawn in and bent like spider's legs. There were men evidently looking like governors, suspended upside down with their hearts pierced with halberts. Some were being flogged with iron rods. Some were being crushed under living rocks. Some were being pecked by weird birds and others were having their throats torn out by poisonous dragons. There were so many varieties of torture suffered by sinners of numerous categories.

The most outstanding of all the horrors, however, was an ox-carriage falling in mid-air grazing the tops of the sword trees that had branches pointed like animals' fangs, through which heaps of bodies of dead souls were spitted. In this carriage, with its bamboo blinds blown upward by the blast of Hell, a court lady as gorgeously dressed as an empress or a princess was writhing in agony, her black hair streaming amidst flames and her white neck bent upward. This figure of the agonizing court lady in the ox-carriage consumed by flames was the most ghostly representation of the thousand and one tortures in the burning Hell. The multifarious horrors in the whole picture were focussed on this one character. It was a master work of such divine inspiration that no one could have looked at her without hearing in his ears the agonizing outcries of the condemned souls in pandemonium.

It was for this reason, indeed, his consuming desire to paint this picture, that the terrible incident occurred. If it had not been for this event, how could even Yoshihide have succeeded in painting that graphic picture of the tortures and agonies in Hell? So he could complete the picture, his life had to come to a miserable end. Indeed, it was to this very Hell in his picture, that Yoshihide, the greatest painter in Japan, had condemned himself.

I am afraid that in my hurry to tell you about this strange hell screen, I have reversed the order of my story. Now my story will return to Yoshihide who was commanded to paint a picture of Hell by the Grand Lord.

VII

For five or six months after that Yoshihide devoted himself to painting the picture on the screen without making even a single courtesy call at the mansion. Isn't it strange that, with all his indulgent love for his daughter, once he took to painting a picture, he had even no thought of seeing her. To borrow the words of his apprentices, he became like a man possessed of a fox. The rumor current at that time had it that he had been able to gain fame and reputation because he offered vows to Reynard the god of Good Fortune.

"For positive proof," some said, "steal a look at him when he is at work, and you can see the shady spirits of foxes thronging all around him."

Once he took up his brush, he forgot everything but his work. Night and day he confined himself to his studio, hardly coming out during daylight. His absorption in his work was most extraordinary when he was painting the hell screen.

Shut up in his studio with the shutters always drawn, he would mix his secret colors, and dressing up his apprentices in various gala costumes or in simple clothes, he would paint them with great care.

But these singular oddities were usual with him. It would not have taken the hell screen to drive him to such extreme eccentricities. While he was working on the painting of his "Five Phases of the Transmigration of Souls," he once came across rotting corpses in a street. Then calmly sitting down in front of the malodorous corpses, from which ordinary painters would have turned their eyes aside, he made accurate sketches, at his ease, of the rotting faces and limbs, exact to a single hair. I am afraid that what I have told you does not convey to you a clear idea of his extreme absorption. I cannot, at this time, tell you the particulars, but I will tell you some of the notable instances.

Once one of his boy apprentices had been mixing colors when he said abruptly, "Now I want to have a rest. For some days I've had some bad dreams."

"Indeed, sir?" the apprentice answered formally without interrupting his work. This was not unusual with his master.

"By the way," the artist said, making a rather modest request, "I want you to sit at my bedside while I'm resting."

"All right, sir," the apprentice replied, as he expected that it would be no trouble at all, although he thought it strange that his master should worry over his bad dreams.

"Come along with me into my inner room. Even if any other apprentice should come, don't let him come in," the master ordered hesitatingly, still looking worried. His inner room meant his studio.

On that occasion, as usual, his studio was closely shut up, dim lights burning as if it were night. Around the sides of the room was set up the screen, on which only the rough sketch was done in charcoal. Entering there, the artist went to sleep calmly as if he were dead tired. But he had not been asleep half an hour when an indescribably weird voice came to the apprentice's ears.

VIII

At first it was only a voice. But presently it turned gradually into disconnected words groaned out like a drowning man under water. "What? Do you tell me to come? . . . Where to? . . . Come where to? . . . Who is it that says, 'Come to Hell. Come to the burning Hell.' Whoever is this? Who could it be but . . . ?"

The apprentice forgot about mixing colors,

[47]

and took a furtive look at his master's face. The wrinkled face had turned pale, oozing large drops of perspiration. His mouth was wide open as if gasping for breath, with his sparse teeth showing between dry lips. The thing, moving briskly in his mouth as if pulled by a string or a wire, was his tongue. Disconnected words, of course, came out of his mouth. "H'm, it's you. I expected it might be you . . . Have you come to meet me? . . . So, come. Come to Hell. In Hell my daughter is waiting for me."

The apprentice was petrified with fear, a chill running all over his whole frame, as his eyes seemed to catch sight of an obscure, weird phantom coming down close by the screen. He put his hand on Yoshihide at once, and with all his might tried to shake him out of the clutch of the nightmare. But, in a trance, his master continued to talk to himself and would not wake up. So the apprentice was bold enough to splash the water in the palette on to his master's face.

"I'll be waiting for you, so come by this carriage . . . Take this carriage to Hell." These words, strangled in his throat, had scarcely come out in the form of a groan when Yoshihide sprang up all of a sudden as though he had been stuck with a needle. The evil spirits in his nightmare must still have been hanging heavily upon his eyelids. For a moment he stared into space with his mouth still wide open. Then returning to himself, he ordered curtly, "It's all right now. Go away, will you?"

If the apprentice had made any expostulation, he would surely have been sharply rebuked. So he hurriedly left his master's room. When he came out into the genial outdoor sunshine, he felt relieved as if he had awakened from his own nightmare.

But that was not the worst. A month later another apprentice was called into his studio. Yoshihide, who had been biting his brush, turned on him and said, "I must ask you to strip yourself bare." As the artist had given this kind of order once in a while, the apprentice immediately took off his clothes.

"I haven't seen anyone bound in chains and so, I'm sorry, but will you do as I tell you for a while?" Yoshihide said coldly, with a very strange frown on his face, without any air of being sorry for him. The apprentice was by nature a young man of such burly physique that he could have wielded a sword more adroitly than a brush. Nevertheless, he was astonished beyond measure, and in his later reference to the occasion, he repeatedly remarked, "Then I was afraid that the master had gone mad and that he was going to kill me." Yoshihide felt impatient at his hesitation. Producing iron chains from somewhere, he sprang on his back, and peremptorily wrenching his arms, he bound them

tightly. Then he gave a sudden pull at one end of
the chain with such cruel force that the apprentice
was thrown plump on the floor by the sudden im-
pact of the strong pull and the unendurable grip
of the chain.

IX

The apprentice at that time looked just like a
wine keg rolled over on its side. All his limbs were
so cruelly bent and twisted that he could move
nothing but his head. The arrest of the circulation
of his blood under the tension of the chain turned
the color of his skin, his face, chest and limbs livid
in no time. However, Yoshihide, gave no heed to
his pain in the least, and walking about his chained
body he made many sketches. It is quite needless
to tell you what dreadful torture the apprentice
suffered under the tight bondage.

If nothing had happened at the moment, his
sufferings might have continued. Fortunately—it
might rather be more appropriate to say unfortunately—after a while, a slender strip of something
flowed gleaming up to the tip of the nose of the
apprentice, who, overcome with fright, drew in his
breath and screamed, "A snake! A snake!"

The apprentice told me that he had felt as if all
the blood in his body would freeze at once. The
snake was actually on the point of touching with
its cold tongue the flesh of his neck into which

the chain was biting. At this unexpected occurrence, the cold-blooded Yoshihide must have been startled. Hurriedly casting away his brush, he bent down, and catching the snake by the tail, he dangled it head downward. Suspended, the snake lifted its head and coiled itself around its own body, but could not reach Yoshihide's hand.

"Go to hell, you damned snake! You've marred a good stroke." In exasperation, Yoshihide dropped the snake into the jar in the corner of the room, and reluctantly undid the chain that bound the apprentice's body. But he did nothing more than to unchain the poor apprentice without even offering a single word of apology or sympathy. For him, his failure in that one stroke must have been a matter of greater regret than to have his apprentice bitten by the snake. Later I was told that he kept the snake for the express purpose of making sketches of it.

To hear of these episodes, you will be able to form a good idea of Yoshihide's mad and sinister absorption. In conclusion let me tell you another story of how a thirteen to fourteen year old apprentice met with such a dreadful experience that it nearly cost him his life during the painting of the Hell Screen. He was a fair-complexioned boy with a girlish face. One night he happened to be called to Yoshihide's room, when in the lamplight he saw his master feeding a strange bird a piece of raw meat which lay in the palm of his hand. The bird was the size of a house cat. It had big, round, amber-colored eyes and ear-shaped feathers jutting out from both sides of its head, and looked extraordinarily like a cat.

X

Yoshihide by nature hated any external interference in whatever he did. As was the case with the snake, he did not let his apprentices know what he planned to do. Sometimes on his desk were placed human skulls, and at other times silver bowls or lacquered tableware. The surprising things he set out on his desk varied according to what he was painting. Nobody could ever find out where he kept these things. For one thing, such circumstances must have lent force to the rumor widely afloat at that time that he was under the divine protection of the Great Goddess of Fortune. So when the apprentice caught sight of the strange creature, he thought that it must also be one of the models for his picture of Hell on the screen, and asked, "What do you wish, sir?" bowing respectfully before his master.

"Look, how tame it is!" the painter said, licking his red lips, as if he had not heard the question.

"What's the name of this creature, sir? I've

never seen one like this." With these words, the apprentice stared at the cat-like bird with ears sticking out as if it were something sinister.

"What? Never seen anything like this? That's the trouble with town-bred folks. They ought to know better. It's a bird called a horned owl. A huntsman from Kurama [7] gave it to me a few days ago. I assure you there aren't many as tame as this."

So saying, he slowly raised his hand and stroked the feathers on the back of the horned owl which had just eaten up the good meat. Just at that moment the bird, with a shrill menacing screech, suddenly flew up from the desk, and with the talons of both feet outstretched pounced upon the apprentice. At that instance had he not raised his sleeve and hid his face in it, he would have been badly wounded. Screaming in fright, he tried frantically to drive away the horned owl. But the big bird, taking advantage of his unguarded moments, continued to click its beak and peck at him. The boy, forgetting the presence of his master, had to run up and down the room in confusion, standing up to defend himself, and sitting down to drive it away. The bird followed him closely and during unguarded moments would dart at his eyes. The fierce flapping of its wings brought on some mysterious effects, like the smell of fallen leaves, the spray of a water-

[7] "Kurama" is a village in the suburbs of Kyoto.

fall, or the odor of soured monkey-wine.[8] The apprentice felt so helpless that the dim oil light looked like a misty moonlight, and his master's very room an ominous, ghastly valley in the depths of the remote mountains.

However, it was not only the horned owl's attacks that overwhelmed the apprentice with terror. What sent the horror of despair into his heart was the sight of Yoshihide. All this while his master had been coolly watching this tragic uproar and had been leisurely sketching, on a piece of paper which he had deliberately unrolled, this ghastly scene of the girlish boy tortured and disfigured by the sinister bird. When the poor boy out of the corner of his eye caught sight of what his master was doing, a shudder of deathly horror ran through his whole frame, and he expected every moment that he was going to be killed by him.

XI

As a matter of fact, it was possible that his master might have planned to kill him, for he deliberately called the apprentice that night to carry out his diabolical scheme to set the horned owl on the handsome boy and paint him running about in terror. So the instant the boy saw what his master's design was, he involuntarily hid his face in both

8 "Monkey-wine" is a wine produced by the natural fermentation of grapes collected by monkeys.

his sleeves, and after a wild, indescribable scream, he collapsed at the foot of the sliding-door in the corner of the room. Just at that moment, something tumbled down with a loud crash. Then all of a sudden the horned owl's flapping of its wings became more violent than ever, and Yoshihide, giving a startled outcry, seemed to have risen to his feet. Terrified out of his wits, the apprentice raised his head to see what was the matter. The room had turned pitch dark, and out of the darkness his master's harsh irritated voice calling for his apprentice fell upon his ears.

Presently there was a distant response by one of his apprentices, who hurriedly came in with a light. The sooty light showed that the rush-light stand had been knocked down and that a pool of the spilt oil had formed on the mats, where the horned owl was found tossing about in pain, flapping only one of its wings. Yoshihide, half raising himself, mumbled something understandable to no mortals—and with good reason. A black snake had coiled itself tightly around the body of the horned owl from its neck to one of its wings. This fierce fight had started, presumably because the apprentice overturned the jar as he suddenly crouched, and the cocky horned owl tried to clutch and peck at the snake which had slid out. The two apprentices, exchanging glances in open-mouthed amazement, had been watching this thrilling battle for a while before they bowed humbly to their master and crept out of the room. No one knows what became of the horned owl and the snake after that.

There were many other instances of this kind. As I told you before, it was at the beginning of fall that he was ordered by the Grand Lord to paint the picture of Hell on the screen. From then on to the end of the winter, the apprentices were under constant danger from their master's mysterious behavior. Toward the end of the winter Yoshihide came to some deadlock in his work on the screen. He became gloomier than ever and noticeably harsher in speech. He could make no progress in the rough sketch, of which he had completed eighty percent. He appeared so dissatisfied that he might not have hesitated even to blot out the rough sketch.

No one could tell what the trouble was, with the picture on the screen. Neither did anyone care to find out. The apprentices, who had learned at their bitter cost by past experience, took all possible means to keep away from their master as though they felt that they were in the same cage with a tiger or a wolf.

XII

Accordingly, for the time being there had been no occurrence worthy of a special mention. All that deserves some notice is that Yoshihide, the obstinate old man, somehow became so strangely maudlin that he was sometimes found weeping when there was no one near. One day when one of the apprentices went out into the garden, he found his master, with his eyes full of tears, looking vacantly into the sky which indicated that spring was not a long while off. More ashamed and embarrassed than his master, the apprentice crept away from his presence without saying a word. Is it not strange that a stout-hearted old man who took up roadside corpses as models for his sketches should weep like a child because he could not find a suitable subject to paint on the screen?

While Yoshihide was so totally absorbed in painting the picture on the screen somehow or other his daughter gradually became so gloomy that it became evident to us that she was trying to hold back her tears. As she was a modest fair-complexioned girl with a quiet composed face, she looked all the more lonely and disconsolate, with her tearful eyes overshadowed by her heavy eye-lashes. At first various guesses were made, such as "She is always absorbed in her thoughts, missing her father and mother," "She is love-sick," and so on. However, in the course of time the rumor began to spread that the Grand Lord was trying to force his desire on her. From that time on, the people stopped talking about the girl as if they had completely forgotten about her affair.

It was just about this time that late one night I was passing by the corridor alone when suddenly the monkey Yoshihide came bounding up to me and persistently pulled me by the hem of my skirt. If I remember rightly, it was a mild night bathed in such mellow moonlight as one might have felt was laden with the fragrance of sweet plum blossoms. In the moonlight I could see the monkey baring his white teeth, with wrinkles on the tip of his nose, and screaming wildly as if it had gone mad. I felt thirty percent uncanny and seventy percent angry, and at first I wanted to give him a kick and pass by. But on reflection, I thought of the instance of the "samurai" who had incurred the displeasure of the young Lord by chastising the monkey. However, the monkey's behavior suggested that something out of the ordinary might have happened. So I walked aimlessly for a dozen yards toward the direction in which he pulled me.

I took a turn around the corridor and came as far as the side, which opened up, through the graceful branches of the pine tree, a fine vista of the broad expanse of the pond sparkling like crystals in the night. Then my ears were arrested by the sounds of a confused fight in the room near by. All around it was as still as a graveyard, and in a faint light that was half moonlight and half haze, nothing was to be heard but the splashing of the fish. Instinctively I stopped and went stealthily up to the outside of the sliding-doors ready to deal them a blow if they proved to be rioters.

XIII

The monkey Yoshihide must have been impatient of my actions. Whining as pitifully as if his neck were being strangled, he scampered around my legs a couple of times and then suddenly bounded up on my shoulders. Instinctively I turned my head aside to dodge being clawed, while the monkey clung to the sleeve of my robe so as not to slip down. On the spur of the moment, I involuntarily staggered back a few steps and bumped against the sliding-door. Then I had not a moment to hesitate. I abruptly threw open the door and was about to rush on into the inner part of the room outside the reach of the moonlight. Then to my alarm, my sight was barred by a young woman who came dashing out of the room as if projected by a spring. In her impetuosity she very nearly bumped into me and tumbled down outside the room. I could not tell why, but she knelt down there and looked up into my face, out of breath, shuddering all over as if she were still seeing something frightful.

I need not take the trouble to tell you that she was Yoshihide's daughter. But that night she looked so extraordinarily attractive that her image was indelibly branded upon my eyes as if she were a changed being. Her eyes were sparkling brightly, her cheeks in a rosy glow. Her dishevelled skirt and undergarment added to her youthful bloom and irresistible charm quite unlike the innocent girl that she was. Was this really the painter's daughter who was so delicate and modest in every way? Supporting myself against the door, I watched the beautiful girl in the moonlight. Then suddenly aware of the flurried footsteps of a man receding into the dark, as if I could point him out, I asked, "Who is it?"

The girl, biting her lips, only shook her head silently. She appeared to feel deep chagrin.

So stooping down, I put my mouth to her ear and asked, "Who was it?" in a low voice. But still she shook her head again and made no answer. With the tips of her eyelashes full of tears, she was biting her lips harder than ever.

On account of my inborn stupidity, I can understand nothing but what is as clear as day. So not knowing what to say, I remained rooted to the spot, as if I were intent on listening to the thumping of the girl's heart. For one thing, I could not find it in my heart to question her any more.

I don't know how long I waited thus. However, shutting the door which I had left open, I looked back toward the girl who seemed to have recovered a little from her agitation, and as gently as possible said to her, "Now go back to your room."

[60]

Troubled with an uneasiness of mind for having seen something which I should not have, and feeling ashamed—of whom I did not know—I began to walk back to where I had come from. But I had not walked ten steps before someone behind me timidly pulled me by the hem of my skirt. In surprise, I looked back. Who do you think it was?

It was the monkey Yoshihide, repeatedly bowing his head to express his gratitude with his hands on the ground like a man, his gold bell tinkling.

XIV

One day two weeks later Yoshihide the painter presented himself at the Grand Lord's mansion and begged his personal audience. The Lord, to whom access was ordinarily difficult, was pleased to grant him an audience, and ordered him to be immediately brought before his presence, probably because the painter was in the Lord's good graces, although he was a man of humble station. The painter, as usual, was wearing a yellow robe and soft head gear. Wearing a more sullen look than usual, he respectfully prostrated himself in the Lord's presence. By and by raising his head, he said in a hoarse voice.

"May it please your Lordship if I tell you about the picture of Hell on the screen which you were previously pleased to order me to paint. I have applied myself to the painting night and day, and have very nearly completed the work."

"Congratulations! I am pleased to hear it." However, the Grand Lord's voice was lacking in conviction.

"No, my Lord. Congratulations are not in order," Yoshihide said, lowering his voice, as if he were plagued with dissatisfaction. "It is mostly finished, but there is one thing I am unable to paint."

"What! Is there anything you can't paint?"

"Yes, my Lord. As a rule, I can't paint anything but what I have seen. Otherwise, however hard I try, I can't paint to my satisfaction. This amounts to the same thing as my being unable to paint it."

"Now that you are to paint Hell, you mean you must see it, eh?" A scornful smile crept across the Grand Lord's face.

"You are right, my Lord. A few years ago when there was a big fire, I could see with my own eyes a burning hell of raging flames. That was why I could paint the picture of the God of Twisting Flames. Your Lordship is also acquainted with that picture."

"How about criminals? You haven't yet seen prisoners, have you?" The Grand Lord followed with question upon question as if he had not heard what Yoshihide said.

"I have seen men bound in iron chains. I have made detailed sketches of those tormented by ominous birds. Nor would I say that I am not acquainted with criminals under tortures, and prisoners . . ." Here Yoshihide gave an uncanny grin. "Asleep or awake, they have appeared in my eyes ever so often. Almost every night and day bull-headed demons, horse-headed demons, or three-faced six-armed demons harrow and torment me, clapping their noiseless hands and opening their voiceless mouths. Not those am I anxious or able to paint."

Yoshihide's words must have been a great surprise to the Grand Lord. After fixing his irritated glare into Yoshihide's face for a while, the Lord spat out, "Then what is it you can't paint?" with a disdainful look, knitting his eyebrows.

XV

"I am anxious to paint a nobleman's magnificent carriage falling in mid-air in the very center of the screen," Yoshihide said, and then for the first time fixed his sharp look full on the Lord's face.

I had once heard that when speaking about pictures, the fellow would become as though insane. Certainly there was some such frightful look in his eyes when he spoke out.

"Allow me to describe the carriage," the painter went on. "In this vehicle, an elegant court lady, amidst raging flames, writhes in the agony of pain, with her black hair hanging loose about her shoulders. Choked with a heavy black smoke, her face is turned up toward the roof of the carriage, with her brow tightly drawn. Around the carriage a score or more of ominous birds fly about, clicking their beaks . . . Oh, how can I ever paint such a court lady in the burning carriage?"

"Hm . . . and what? . . ." Strangely enough, the Grand Lord urged Yoshihide to go on with his talk as if he were well pleased.

"Oh, I can't paint it," Yoshihide said once again in a dreary tone, his feverish red lips trembling. But suddenly he changed his attitude, and in dead earnest, made a bold and feverish request in a spirited and snappish tone, "Please, my Lord, burn a nobleman's carriage before my eyes, and if possible, . . ."

The Grand Lord darkened his face for an instant but suddenly burst into a peal of laughter.

"All your wishes shall be granted," the Grand Lord declared, his voice half choked with his laughter. "Don't take the trouble to inquire about the possibility."

His words struck horror into my heart. It may have been my presentiment. Anyway the Grand Lord's behavior on that occasion was most extraordinary, as though it had been infected with Yoshihide's madness. White froth was gathering at the corner of his mouth, and his eyebrows twitched violently.

"Yes, I will burn up a nobleman's carriage." As he paused, his incessant heavy laughter went on. "A charming woman dressed up like a court lady shall ride in the carriage. Writhing amidst the deadly flames and black smoke, the lady in the carriage will die in agony. Your suggestion of finding such a model for your picture does you full credit as the greatest painter in the whole country. I praise you. I praise you highly."

At the Grand Lord's words, Yoshihide had turned pale and had been trying to move his lips for perhaps a minute when he put his hands on the matted floor as if all his muscles had relaxed, and said politely, "I am most grateful to you, my Lord," in a voice so low as to be hardly audible.

This was probably because, with the Grand Lord's words, the horror of the scheme which he had had in mind vividly flashed across his mind. Only this once in my life did I think of Yoshihide as a pitiful creature.

XVI

One night a few days later, according to his promise, the Grand Lord summoned Yoshihide to witness the burning of a nobleman's carriage right before his eyes. However, this did not take place on the grounds of the Grand Lord's mansion of

[65]

Horikawa. It was burned at his villa in the hilly suburbs commonly called the mansion of Yuge (Snow-thaw) where his sister had once lived.

This residence had been uninhabited for a long time, and the spacious gardens had fallen into a state of dilapidation. In those days many uncanny rumors were going around about the late sister of the Grand Lord. Some said that on moonless nights her mysterious scarlet-colored skirts would be seen moving along the corridors without touching the floor. Without doubt, these rumors must have been wild guesses started by those who had seen the complete desertion of the mansion. But there is nothing to wonder at in the circulation of these rumors, for the whole neighborhood was so lonely and desolate even in the daytime that after dark even the murmuring of the water running through the gardens added all the more to the dismal gloom, and the herons flying about in the starlight might naturally have been taken for ominous birds.

On that night it was pitch dark with no moonlight. The rushlights showed that the Grand Lord, dressed in a bright green garment and a dark violet skirt, was seated near the verandah. He was sitting cross-legged on a rush mat hemmed with white brocade. Before and behind him and at the right and left of him, five or six samurai stood in respectful attendance upon him. One of them stood out with prominent conspicuousness. A few years before, during the campaign in the Tohoku District, he had eaten human flesh to allay his hunger. That gave him such herculean strength that he could tear the horn of a live deer apart. Clad in armor, he stood in full dignity beneath the verandah with the tip of his sheathed sword turned upward. The lurid ghastliness of the scene, turning bright and dark under the lights which flickered in the night wind, made me wonder whether I was dreaming or awake.

Presently when a magnificent carriage was drawn up into the garden to make its commanding appearance in the dark, with long shafts placed on its chassis and its gold metalwork and fittings glittering like so many stars, we felt a chill come over us, although it was spring. The interior of the carriage was heavily enclosed with blue blinds, of which the hems were embroidered in relief, so we could not tell what was inside. Around the carriage a number of menials, each with a blazing torch in hand, waited attentively, worrying over the smoke which drifted toward the verandah.

Yoshihide was on his knees on the ground facing the verandah just in front of the Lord. Dressed in a cream-colored garment and soft head-gear, he looked smaller and homelier than usual, as though he had been stunted under the oppressive atmosphere of the starry sky. The man squatting behind him, dressed in a similar garment, was presumably his apprentice. As they were some way off in the dark, even the colors of their garments were not clearly discernible.

XVII

The time was very near midnight. Darkness, enveloping the grove and stream, seemed to listen silently to the breathing of all those present. Meanwhile the passage of the gentle wind wafted the sooty smell of the torches toward us. The Grand Lord had been silently watching this extraordinary scene for a while when he stepped forward and called sharply, "Yoshihide."

Yoshihide seemed to say something in reply, but what my ears could catch sounded nothing more than a groan.

"Tonight I'm going to set fire to the carriage as you wish," the Grand Lord said, looking askance at his attendants. Then I saw the Grand Lord exchange a significant glance with his attendants. But this might have been my fancy. Yoshihide seemed to have raised his head reverently, but did not say anything.

"There, behold! That's the carriage in which I usually ride. Yoshihide, you know it, don't you? Now according to your wish, I am going to set fire to it and bring to life a blazing hell on earth before your very eyes."

The Lord paused again, and again exchanging

significant looks with his attendants, he proceeded in a displeased tone.

"In the carriage is a woman criminal—bound in chains. If it is fired, I am sure that she will have her flesh roasted and her bones scorched, and that she will writhe in dire agony to death. No better model can you have for the completion of your picture. Don't miss seeing her snow-white skin burned and charred. Watch closely her black hair dance up in the infernal sparks of fire."

The Grand Lord closed his mouth for the third time. I do not know what came to his mind. Then shaking his shoulders in silent laughter, he said, "The sight will be handed down to posterity. I will also watch it here now. There, raise the blinds and let Yoshihide see the woman inside."

At his command, one of the menials, holding aloft a pine torch in one hand, strode up to the carriage, and stretching out his free hand, he quickly raised the blinds. The red blazing light from his torch waved wildly with a crackling noise, and suddenly lightened up the small interior with dazzling brightness, revealing a woman cruelly bound in chains on the seat. Oh, whoever could have mistaken her? Although she was dressed up in a gorgeously embroidered silken "kimono" with a cherry-blossom design, gold hair-pins shining with a brilliant glitter in her hair which hung loose about her shoulders, the fact that she was

Yoshihide's daughter was in unmistakable evidence in her trim, maidenly form, her lovely charming profile of graceful modesty. I very nearly gave an outcry.

At that moment the samurai who stood opposite me roused himself and cast a sharp glance at Yoshihide, with his hand on the hilt of his sword. In amazement, I looked toward Yoshihide, who seemed to have been startled out of his wits. Although he had been on his knees, he instantly sprang to his feet, and stretching out his arms, he unconsciously attempted to rush toward the carriage.

However, as he was off in the dark background, I could not discern his face clearly. But that was the matter of a passing moment. For all at once, his face which had turned sheet-white came vividly into view through the intervening shadow of the night, while his body seemed to have been lifted up into space by some invisible power. Just then at the Grand Lord's command, "Set fire!" a shower of torches thrown in by the menials bathed the carriage in a flood of lurid light and set it ablaze in a pillar of raging flames.

XVIII

The fire enveloped the whole chassis in no time. The instant the purple tassels on the roof, fanned by the sudden wind, waved upward, volumes of smoke spiraled up against the blackness of the night, and such furious sparks of fire danced up in mid-air that the bamboo blinds, the hangings on both sides, and the metal fittings on the roof, bursting into so many balls of fire, shot up skyward. The bright color of the tongues of the raging fire, which soared up far into the sky, looked like celestial flames spurting out of the orb of heaven which had fallen down to the earth. A moment before I had very nearly cried out, but now I was so completely stunned and dumbfounded with mouth agape I could do nothing but watch this terrible spectacle in a daze. But as for the father, Yoshihide. . . .

Still now I can remember how the painter Yoshihide looked at that moment. He attempted to rush toward the carriage in spite of himself. But the instant the fire blazed up, he stopped, and with his arms outstretched as if magnetized, he fastened such a sharp gaze upon the burning chassis as to penetrate the raging flames and heavy smoke which had enveloped the whole carriage. In the flood of light that had bathed his whole body, his ugly wrinkled face was brought into clear view even to the tip of his beard.

His wide open eyes, his distorted lips, and the quivering of his cheeks which constantly twitched, all were tangible expressions of the mixture of dread, grief, and bewilderment which crowded

[71]

upon his mind. Neither a robber who was about to be beheaded nor a heinous criminal who was dragged before the judgment seat of Yuma could have worn a more painful or agonized face. At the sight of him, even the samurai of herculean strength was greatly shocked and respectfully looked up into the Grand Lord's face.

The Grand Lord, however, tightly biting his lips, fixed his gaze upon the carriage, showing a sinister grin from time to time. Inside the carriage —oh, how could I ever have the heart or courage to convey to you a detailed description of the girl in the carriage who flashed into my sight. Her hair, charming face, which, choked with smoke, fell back, and her long alluring hair which came loose while she was trying to shake off the spreading fire, as well as her beautiful, gorgeous kimono with its cherry-blossom pattern which turned into a lambent flame in no time—what a cruel spectacle all this was! By and by a gust of night wind blew away the smoke toward the other side, and when the sparks of fire shot up like gold dust above the raging blaze, she fainted in such convulsive agonies that even the chains which bound her might have burst. Above all others, this atrocious torture of hell itself brought into gruesome reality before our very eyes sent such a blood-curdling shudder through the hearts of all present including the samurai that our hair stood on end.

Then once again we thought that the midnight wind had moaned through the tree-tops. The sound of the wind had scarcely passed into the dark sky—no one knew where to—when something black bounded like a ball without either touching the ground or flying through the air, and plunged straight from the roof of the mansion into the furiously blazing carriage. Amidst the burned crimson-lacquered lattice which was crumbling in pieces, it put its hands on the warped shoulders of the girl, and gave, out of the screens of black smoke, a long and piercing shriek of intense grief like the tearing of silk, then again two or three successive screams.

Involuntarily we gave a unanimous outcry of surprise. What was holding fast to the shoulders of the dead girl, with the red curtain of blazing flames behind it, was the monkey, which went by the nickname of Yoshihide at the mansion of Horikawa.

XIX

But it was only for a few seconds that the monkey remained in our sight. The instant the sparks shot up like thousands of shooting stars into the night air, the girl together with the monkey sank to the bottom of the whirling black smoke. After that, in the midst of the garden, nothing else was to be seen but the carriage of fire blazing with a terrific noise. A pillar of fire might have been a more appropriate phrase to describe the turbulent, furious flames which shot up into the dark starry sky.

In front of the pillar of fire, Yoshihide stood still, rooted to the ground. What a wonderful transfiguration he had undergone! A mysterious radiance, a kind of blissful ecstasy showed on the wrinkled face of Yoshihide who had been agonized by the tortures of hell until a minute before. His arms were tightly crossed on his chest as if he had forgotten that he was in the presence of the Grand Lord. No longer did his eyes seem to mirror the image of his daughter's agonized death. His eyes seemed to delight beyond measure in the beautiful color of the flame and the form of the woman writhing in her last infernal tortures.

The wonder was not limited to his ecstatic transport with which he was watching the death agony of his beloved daughter. Yoshihide at that moment revealed something that was not human, some such mysterious dignity as King Lion's wrath which you might see in your dreams. It may have been our imagination. But in our eyes, even the flocks of night birds, which, startled by the unexpected fire, screeched and clamored around, seemed to fly shy of the soft head-gear of Yoshihide. Even the eyes of the soulless birds seemed to be aware of a mysterious dignity which shone over his head like a halo.

Even the birds appeared like that. Much more did we quake within, with bated breath, watching Yoshihide closely and intently, our hearts overwhelmed with such awe and reverence as if we looked up to a newly made Buddhist image at its unveiling ceremony. The fire and smoke of the carriage which had spread all around with a roaring sound and Yoshihide who stood captivated and petrified there by the spectacle inspired our horror-stricken hearts, for the moment, with a mysterious awe and solemnity beyond all description. However, the Grand Lord, harrowed by the very horror of the scene, appeared pale and livid as though he were a changed being. Foam gathering at his mouth, he gasped like a thirsty animal, grasping the knee of his purple-colored skirt tightly with both hands.

XX

The report of the Grand Lord's burning of the carriage spread far and wide—heaven only knows who started it. The first and foremost question that would naturally arise in your mind would be what led the Grand Lord to burn alive Yoshihide's daughter. A variety of guesses were made about the cause. Most people accepted the rumor that his motive was to carry out his vengeance against his thwarted love. But his real underlying intention must have been his design to chastise and correct the perversity of Yoshihide who was anxious to paint the screen even if it involved the burning of a magnificent carriage with the sacrifice of human life. That was what I heard from the Grand Lord's mouth.

Since Yoshihide was eager enough to paint the screen even at the very moment he saw his own daughter burned to death before his eyes, some reviled him as a devil in human shape which felt no scruple about sacrificing his parental love for the sake of his art. The Abbot of Yokawa was one of the staunch supporters of this view, and used to say that, no matter how accomplished one might be in any branch of learning or art, one would have to be condemned to hell, if one were not endowed with the five cardinal virtues of Confucius—benevolence, justice, courtesy, wisdom and fidelity.

A month later when his hell screen was completed, Yoshihide took it immediately to the mansion, and presented it with great reverence to the Grand Lord. The Abbot, who happened to be there at the time, had glared angrily at him from the first, showing a wry face. However, as the screen was unrolled, the high priest must have been struck by the truth of the infernal horrors, the storms of fire ranging from the firmament to the abyss of hell.

"Wonderful!" the Abbot exclaimed in spite of himself, giving an involuntary tap on his knee. Still now I remember how his ejaculation drew a forced smile from the Grand Lord.

From that time on hardly any one, at least in the mansion, spoke ill of the painter, because, strangely enough, no one, including those who harbored the most intense hatred toward Yoshihide, could see the picture on the screen without being struck with its mysterious solemnity or being vividly impressed with its ghastly reality of the exquisite tortures in a burning hell.

However, by that time Yoshihide had already departed this life.

On the night of the day following the completion of his painting of the screen, he hanged himself by putting a rope over the beam of his room. Yoshihide, who survived the untimely death of his only beloved daughter, could no longer find it in his heart to live on in this world.

His body remains buried in the corner of the ruins of his house. However, with the passage of scores of years, wind and rain have worn out the tombstone marking his grave, and overgrowing moss has buried it into oblivion.

A CLOD OF SOIL

IT WAS THE BEGINNING of the tea-picking season
and Osumi was sorely grieved by the loss of her
son, Nitaro, who had been lying practically crippled for over eight years. The death of her son did
not bring unmixed grief to this old widow, whose
soul, the neighbors said, would be born to live
a blessed life in the Land of Bliss after her death.
When she burned an incense stick to pray for the
peaceful repose of his soul now laid in his coffin,
she felt as if she had at last managed to cross the
steep mountain pass.

After the funeral service of Nitaro was over, the
first question that came up was what should be
done with his wife, Otami, and her little son. This
young widow had taken upon herself most of the
family farm work from the hands of her husband
who was bedridden. If she left, the family would
be burdened not only with the care of the little
child but would have no means left for earning a
living. Osumi had a good mind to seek a husband
for the widowed Otami after the lapse of forty-

nine [1] days and to have her work for the family as she did when he was living. In her heart she thought that her late son's cousin, Yokichi, might be a suitable husband for the young widow.

"Are you thinking of leaving this child and me already? It's wrong of me to have been silent about a plan for your future," extraordinarily shocked, Osumi asked in a tone of more appeal than reprimand when she saw Otami tidying up the room on the morning of the eighth day after the death of her husband. Osumi was looking after the grandchild on the verandah adjoining the back room. The plaything she gave him was a spray of cherry-blossoms in full bloom which she had taken from the school playground.

"What are you talking about?" Otami answered with a smile, without even looking at her. What a relief it was to Osumi.

"I just imagined so. Sure you're not leaving us, are you?" Osumi kept harping on her solicitous entreaty in a whining voice. Presently her own words made her sentimental, until tears flowed freely down her cheeks.

"Why, really I mean to stay here for good, if you wish." Otami also grew tearful before she was aware of it, and took up her child, Koji, on her

[1] In Japan a common Buddhist superstition goes that the soul of a dead person departs his house forty-nine days after his death.

lap. "I've got this child. Why should I ever go any-where else?" Koji, looking strangely shy, appeared attracted to the spray of cherry-blossoms lying upon the old mat of the back room.

* * * * * * *

Otami kept on working as hard as she did while Nitaro was living. However, the problem of her taking a husband could not be as easily settled as had been expected. She did not seem to have any interest at all in this matter. Osumi of course took every opportunity to arouse Otami's interest in her remarriage and to approach her with a proposal. However, Otami gave only evasive answers like "Maybe next year, please." Doubtless this was as much a joy as a worry to Otami, who finally decided to wait for the turn of the year, yielding to her daughter-in-law's wishes. However, she took seriously to heart what other people might think of them.

The following year came and Otami seemed to give no thought to anything but working out in the fields. The old woman began more persistently and even prayerfully to persuade the young widow to take a husband. This was partly because she worried over criticism leveled by her relatives and backbiting by people.

"But you see, you're so young you can't go along without a man for good, I'm afraid," appealed Osumi.

"Good heavens!" answered Otami. "Can't I get along without a man? How can I help it? If you bring in a stranger among us, Hiro will have a hard time, you'll be under pressure, and I'll have no end of cares and troubles."

"This is why I urge you. Take Yokichi for your husband, won't you? He's given up gambling forever, I understand," persuaded Osumi.

"Why, he's a relative of yours, but, after all, he's a stranger to me," replied the younger woman.

"But you'll have to be patient for years and years," Osumi argued.

"Why not? It's for the sake of my dear Hiro. If I only suffer now, the whole of our farm will pass undivided into his hands." Otami thoughtfully replied.

"Well," Osumi said lowering her voice, as she always did when she talked of this matter. "In any case people will talk, you see. I pray you, Otami, tell others exactly what you've just said to me."

How often they had questions and answers like these! But each time only added to the strength of Otami's determination. Really, without the help of a male hand, she worked harder than ever, planting potatoes and reaping barley. Moreover, during the summers she kept cows, and even on rainy days she went out mowing. This hard work was in itself her strong resistance against admitting a stranger into her home. At last Osumi gave up the idea of getting a husband for Otami. However, her resignation was not altogether unpleasant to her.

*   *   *   *   *   *   *

Otami continued to support the family by her own hands. There was no doubt that her toil was motivated by her whole-hearted desire to work for the sake of her little son, Hiro. Another more inherent cause was traceable to the power of heredity that ran deep in her blood. She was a daughter of a so-called migrant family that had formerly moved into this district from a sterile mountainous province.

"Your Otami is much stronger than she looks," from time to time the next-door old woman was heard to say to Osumi. "The other day I saw her carrying four huge bundles of rice-plants on her back."

Osumi tried to translate her thanks to Otami by taking over the management of the daily household chores: looking after her grandson, taking care of the cows, cooking meals, washing clothes, going to the neighbor's house to draw water, etc. Bent with age, she found happiness and pleasure in taking over all sorts of household tasks herself.

One night in the late autumn, Otami came home with difficulty, carrying bulky bundles of pine-needles under her arms. Just then Osumi with Hiroji fastened to her back, was stoking a fire in the furnace in a corner of the small earthen floor.

"You must be cold. You're back late," Osumi said.

"I did a bit of extra work today," Otami replied wearily.

Tossing down the bundles of pine-needles below the sill, without even taking off her muddy straw sandals, she came in and sat down right by the side of the open fireplace, where an oak stump was burning with a cheery flame. Osumi tried to rise to her feet at once, but burdened with Hiroji on her back, she had to hold on to the edge of the bathtub before she could slowly raise herself.

"Have a bath right away, won't you?"

"I'm too hungry for a bath. I'd rather eat sweet potatoes first. You've got some boiled sweet potatoes, haven you?"

Osumi toddled along to the sill, and brought back the pot of boiled sweet potatoes. "I've had them waiting for you for a long time. I'm afraid they're cold now."

They roasted the sweet potatoes over the fire in the open fireplace.

"Hiro's fast asleep. Lay the tot in bed."

"No, it's so awfully cold tonight and he won't go to sleep," Osumi replied.

While she talked, Otami began cramming her mouth full of the sweet potatoes which had begun to steam. Her manner of eating could only be observed among farmers who come back home after the day's tiresome labors. She ravenously gulped down one sweet potato after another which she had removed from the spit. Osumi, feeling the weight of the faintly snoring Hiroji on her back, busily kept broiling more sweet potatoes.

"Anyway working as hard as you do, you must feel twice as hungry as anyone else." Time and again Osumi looked admiringly into the face of Otami, as she kept cramming the sweet potatoes into her mouth in the dim light of the sooty fire.

* * * * * * *

Otami toiled on all the harder doing a man's work without sparing herself. Sometimes even at night she walked around, thinning out greens by the light of a lantern. Osumi always had respect for her daughter-in-law. Really it was more a sense of awe than respect. Except for labor in the fields and hills, Otami thrust all work upon her mother-in-law, without washing even her own clothes. Nevertheless, without breathing a word of complaint, Osumi worked on, straightening herself up now and then.

Osumi never saw the old woman next door without extolling her daughter-in-law to the skies, saying, "Anyway Otami's like that. So no matter when I die, my family will have nothing to worry about."

However, Otami's mania for work seemed too

far gone to be thrown off. When another year had passed she began to speak of extending the sphere of her labor to the mulberry field across the irrigation ditch. She asserted that it was absurd to tenant out the land covering a quarter of an acre for only ten dollars a year. She went on to reason that if they planted mulberry trees there and raised silkworms at odd times, their labor would be sure to yield them about 150 dollars net yearly, barring fluctuations in the silkworm market. Although money was their greatest consideration, it was more than Osumi could bear to be pressed with extra labor. Above all, raising silkworms would be an exacting demand upon their time and far beyond the limit of her capacity and endurance. At last she offered a querulous remonstrance.

"You see, Otami. I'm not shirking. We haven't got a man—just a little crying child to look after. Even now the work is too much for me. So your idea's too absurd. How could I ever take up raising silkworms? Think of me a little. I pray you!"

In the face of her mother-in-law's plaintive protest, Otami did not have the heart to insist on having her own way. So she gave up the idea of raising silkworms, but insisted on carrying her point in planting the mulberry field.

"Never mind. Only I've got to work out in the fields." Casting a determined look at Osumi, she grumbled out an insinuating remark.

From this time on, Osumi again thought of adopting a son. Formerly she had entertained this idea out of her anxiety over her family's living and out of her regard for what people might think of her family. But now she wished to adopt a son out of her impatience to be released from her painful duty of taking care of the housework. So now how more intense and irresistible than ever before was her desire to receive a son-in-law into her family!

Just at the time when the tangerine fields were tinged with full-blown blossoms, Osumi seated in front of the oil-lamp, ventured to bring up the proposal, eyeing Otami over the rims of her spectacles, which she wore while doing her needlework at night.

"Talking of my taking a husband again! That's no concern of mine," Otami, sitting cross-legged and munching salted peas, turned a deaf ear. Formerly Osumi might, in all probability, have dropped the proposal.

"But you shouldn't altogether say, 'No,' *now*." This particular night she persistently tried her best to persuade Otami. "Tomorrow at the funeral service of the Miyashita family, our family is assigned the duty of digging the grave. At a time like this I wish we had a man."

"Don't worry. I'll do the digging," Otami interjected.

"Surely not. As you are a woman, you don't

mean it." Osumi thought of laughing it off. But looking into Otami's face, she dared not.

"Granny, you want to retire now, don't you?" Otami, with her hands on the knees of her crossed legs, coldly touched Osumi on her sensitive spot.

"Oh, no, Otami, why should I ever . . . ?" Osumi, who was caught off balance took off her spectacles in spite of herself. But she could not tell why she did so.

"You remember what you said when Hiro's father died, don't you?" persisted Otami. "It would be a sin against our ancestors ever to divide up the estate of our family . . ."

"Well, yes, I said so. But we have to take things as they are. This can't be helped." Osumi tried hard to plead in favor of bringing a man into their family. Nevertheless, her argument did not sound plausible or convincing even to her own ears. First of all, this was because she could not bring up her real underlying motive, that of living an easier life.

"It may be all very well for you, as you'll die earlier than I." Continuing to munch salted peas, Otami, who had discovered Osumi's vulnerability, began taking her severely to task. Her natural glib tongue lent force to her reprimand. "In the situation I'm in, how can I shirk my responsibility? I haven't remained a widow for any show or pride. At night when my limbs are too painful for me to go to sleep, I often feel that it's no good being

[87]

stubborn. But I'm doing all this though, thinking it's for the sake of our family and Hiro."

In a stupid daze, Osumi looked Otami in the face. In the course of time, her mind clearly began to grasp a certain fact. It was that struggle as she might, she could never ease up until she closed her eyes forever. After Otami's outburst was over, she put on her spectacles again.

"But Otami," Osumi concluded her talk as if she were talking to herself. "Things in life don't go only according to reason. Think it over carefully, won't you? I won't say anything more about it."

Twenty minutes later some village youngster walked past the house, singing in a tenor voice:

"The young bride's out on her mowing work today,

Grass bend low, scythe be sharp!"

When the singing died away, Osumi gave another glance at Otami's face over the rims of her spectacles. Otami, on the other side of the lamp, was only yawning heavily, with her legs fully outstretched.

"Now I'll get off to bed. I must get up pretty early in the morning." Muttering these words, Otami snatched a handful of salted peas, and stood up languidly by the fireside.

Osumi silently continued to endure her sufferings for the subsequent three or four years. These were the sufferings an old horse experiences when it teams up with a young spirited one. Otami persevered with her arduous work and toiled in the fields like a bee. To outsiders Osumi seemed to be as happy as ever, taking care of the house. But the shadow of an invisible whip constantly harassed her. She was apt to be scolded or indirectly rebuked by the spirited Otami, sometimes for failing to heat the bath, and at others for forgetting to air unhulled rice or letting the cows out. Nevertheless, without answering back, she continued to endure her sufferings. For one thing, it was because her spirit was accustomed to submission; and for another, because her grandson, Hiro, was attached more to her than to his mother.

Actually to outsiders, Osumi had hardly changed in any way. If she had, it was that she did not praise her son's wife as she had done previously. However, such a trivial change did not attract any special notice from others. At least to the old woman next door, she remained the same blessed woman as ever.

At high noon one summer when the blazing hot sun was beating straight down upon the earth, Osumi was talking with the next-door old woman under the shadow of the grape-vine trellis spreading all over in front of the cow-shed. The old woman talked while smoking cigarette butts. She had carefully collected the cigarette butts left by her son.

"Hm. Otami-san's out mowing hay. She's so young, and yet she does all work without complaining," observed the old woman.

"Well, housework is best for women," responded Osumi.

"No, there's nothing more enjoyable than farming. My son's wife hasn't ever been out weeding much less farming for even a single day in the seven years since they got married. She spends all her days washing her children's clothes and remaking her own."

"Tidying up your children and keeping yourself neat and attractive is an adornment to life," chimed Osumi.

"But the young today don't like to work in the fields. Oh, dear! What's the noise now?" asked the neighbor.

"That noise? Why, it's just the cow breaking wind."

"Oh, the cow breaking wind! Really? When young, it's awful trying to weed, with your back blistered under the scorching rays of the sun," concluded the neighbor.

The two old women generally chatted like that in a familiar and friendly way.

For more than eight years after the death of Jintaro, Otami continued to support her family

single-handed. In the course of time her name had
spread all over the village and beyond. In the eyes
of the villagers, she was no longer a young widow,
who, seized by a mania for work, toiled night and
day. Much less was she a young "missus" to the
village youngsters. Instead she was an example to
all brides. She was a present-day paragon of female
virtue and fidelity. Such spontaneous eulogies were
upon everyone's lips. As for Osumi, she did not
divulge her sufferings or her innermost thoughts
to anyone. Nor did she want to. From the depths
of her heart she placed her faith in Providence,
although she was not clearly conscious of God.
Now that her faith was dashed to pieces, her only
and last hope was her grandson, Hiro. She desperately poured her love out to her darling twelve-
year-old grandson. But this last hope of hers was
often blighted.

One fine fall afternoon Hiro came home hurriedly from school in a state of agitation, holding
a sheaf of books under his arm. Osumi, sitting in
front of the stable, using her knife quite dexter-
ously, was cording persimmons to dry them. He
skipped nimbly over one of the mats, on which
unhulled millet was airing, and smartly arranged
his feet and raised his hand in a crisp salute.

"Granny," he abruptly asked her earnestly, "Is
Mama a very great woman?"

"Why?" Resting her hand which had just been

using the knife, she could not help staring at her grandson's face.

"Because the teacher told us in the morals lesson that she was greater than any other woman in this neighborhood."

"Eh? The teacher? Who?" First she was upset. "Even the school teacher tells my grandson such a shocking lie." Really nothing was a greater surprise to her. After a moment's confusion, she was seized with a fit of anger, and began berating Otami as if she were a changed being.

"That's a lie. A black lie. Your mama works hard only outdoors, so she seems extraordinary and wonderful to others. But she's real wicked at heart. She drives granny hard, and is so headstrong."

Astonished, Hiroji watched his grandmother's face which was livid with anger. In the course of time a reaction must have overtaken her, for she had tears in her eyes.

"So your granny's living with you as her only hope in life. Always keep this in mind. By and by as soon as you're seventeen, get married and let your granny breathe freely. Your mama takes it easy and says you should get married after you're through with your military service. But how could I ever wait that long? You understand. Be doubly kind to granny so as to do your daddy's share of duty, and I'll be very good to you. You shall have everything," Osumi said persuasively.

"Will you give me these persimmons when they're ripe?" Koji was fingering and coveting a basket of persimmons.

"Yes, why not?" Osumi hiccuped her laughter through her tears. "You're just a little tyke, but you understand everything. Now don't change your mind."

The night following this outburst, Osumi had a rowdy squabble with Otami about a trifling matter which arose from Osumi's alleged eating of Otami's share of boiled sweet potatoes. As they became heated in their argument Otami said with a grin, "If you don't want to work, you have no choice but to die."

This incensed Osumi and unexpectedly she raved like an insane woman.

"Hiro, here, wake up!" Osumi aroused Hiroji, who had been asleep all this while with his head on her lap, and continued to howl with rage. "Hiro, wake up! Hiro,—wake up! Listen to what your mama says. She tells me to die. Do you hear? Listen real well, will you? In mama's days we've got a bit more money, but grandpa and granny cleared our three acres of farm and all by ourselves. And yet mama tells me I should die if I want to take things easy . . . Otami, I'll die. Why should I be afraid of dying? I won't be dictated to by you. Oh, I'll die by all means. I'll die and haunt you . . ."

Osumi continued to rave and revile in a loud

voice, holding her grandson who had started to cry in her arms. Otami all this while lay by the fireside, turning a deaf ear to the ravings of Osumi.

*   *   *   *   *   *   *

However, Osumi did not die, while on the other hand Otami, who boasted of her excellent health, caught typhoid fever and died a week later. At that time the disease took an appalling toll of life in the village. The day before she fell ill, she took her turn at the task of digging a grave for the funeral of the iron-smith who had fallen victim to the same disease. At the smith's she saw the young apprentice who was to be sent to the isolation hospital on the very day of the funeral.

"You must've caught it then," after the doctor left, Osumi dropped a hint of her censure to the patient, who lay in bed with her face burning with fever.

The day of Otami's funeral it rained heavily. Nevertheless, her funeral was attended by all the villagers including the village mayor. All those who were there mourned the early death of Otami and expressed their sympathy to Osumi and Hiroji who had lost their breadwinner. The village representative told Osumi that the county office had been contemplating an official commendation for Otami shortly. At these words Osumi could do nothing but bow her head.

"Well, Osumi," went on the good-hearted representative, nodding his bald head. "You'd better resign yourself to your great misfortune. To get the official recommendation of Otami-san, we've sent in petitions to the county office, and I've been there to see the county commissioner five times. But we're going to resign ourselves to the tragedy, so you'd better be resigned, too." His preaching adulterated with levity made the grade-school teachers stare at him with a look of obvious displeasure.

The night after the funeral of Otami found Osumi sleeping with Hiroji inside the same mosquito net in the corner of the back room where the Buddhist alter had been erected. At other times they used to sleep in the room with the light out. That night, however, the altar was still lit with candles and the mats seemed to have been permeated with the peculiar odor of disinfectant, which kept Osumi awake in bed for a long time. Without doubt, Otami's death had at last brought her a great happiness. Now it was no longer necessary for her to work. Besides, she was also free from the fear of being rebuked.

She now had a bank deposit of a thousand dollars and three acres of farmland. She and Hiroji would be free from now on, to eat delicious boiled rice together, instead of having to endure the less-appetizing mixture of boiled barley and rice, and she would also be free to purchase her favorite salted cod by the bale. Never in her life had she felt so relieved from cares as at that moment. Presently her memory vividly recalled a certain night nine years ago. On that night she had heaved the same sigh of relief as she did now. That was the night after the funeral of the only son of her flesh and blood. This was the night on which the funeral of her son's wife who bore her only grandson was also just over.

Osumi opened her eyes of her own accord and found her grandson asleep close by her with his innocent face turned upward. While she was gazing fondly into his relaxed and restful face, it gradually occurred to her that she was a wretched creature and that at the same time both her son, Jintaro, and his wife, Otami, who formed an ill-fated union with her, were also to be pitied. The change in her feelings helped instantly to erase nine years of hatred and bitterness. The parent and her children, all three, were to be pitied. Osumi, who survived the other two to live such a disgraceful life was the most pitiable of them all.

"Otami, why did you die?" she whispered faintly to the departed. Suddenly in spite of herself an endless stream of tears flowed down her cheeks.

After she heard the clock strike four, the sleep of the weary fell upon her, as the sky, over her thatched roof on the eastern horizon was greeting the first chilly grey streaks of dawn.

"NEZUMI-KOZO"—THE JAPANESE ROBIN HOOD

INTRODUCTION

TRADITIONALLY in Japan, Nezumi-Kozo (1795-1832) is accepted as a chivalrous robber who took from the rich to give to the poor, and he may well be called the Robin Hood of Japan. It is generally believed that he was master of *"ninjutsu,"* the art of making oneself invisible and that he carried *nezumi* (mice) in a bag when burgling the mansions of the *daimyo* (feudal lords) and let them loose to deceive awakened sleepers into believing that the noise was caused by mice. In Japanese, *kozo* means apprentice, or urchin.

In the years following the 1868 political revolution which overthrew the Shogunate (feudal government), kabuki plays with Nezumi-Kozo as the hero achieved immense popularity among the Japanese people who had just been emancipated from the yoke of feudalism which for centuries stood upon a hierarchy of four rigid castes in descending order from military, agricultural,

[97]

industrial to commercial. The people, consequently, delighted in any performances which belittled or fooled their former *daimyo* rulers and their parasites who lorded it over the citizens and subjected them to all manner of humiliations and indignities hardly imaginable in present times.

The short story introduced here provides a farcical episode of the Japanese popular traditional hero on the *kabuki* stage.

*   *   *   *   *   *   *

ONE EVENING in early autumn about one hundred and fifty years ago, in an upstairs room of an inn for sailors in Shiodome, Edo,[1] two men who appeared to be gamblers sat talking confidentially for a long time over their cups of sake (rice-wine).

One was a stout dark-complexioned man clad in an unlined kimono, which together with an old-style cloak worn over it, gave his piquantly handsome features a dashing air. The conspicuousness of the tattoo running down to his wrists and his unlined checkered kimono which was done up with a flat silken belt of abacus-bead design coiled round his waist, served to give him the appearance of a degenerate with the touch of a grim rather than foppish trait. His companion, a short, fair

---

[1] "Edo" is the old name of the present capital, Tokyo.

fellow, apparently a cut below him, always addressed the swarthy, thickset man as "Boss." They appeared to be of about the same age and to be on more cordial and congenial terms than ordinary boss and henchman are, as might be readily seen in the easy and familiar manner in which they filled each other's cups.[2]

Although it was an evening of early autumn, the white wall of a warehouse across the street which was still aglow with the warm rays of the setting sun, and the luxuriant foliage of a willow tree ablaze in the evening sunlight, vividly recalled the lingering heat of the late summer. A waft of wind coming at times over the sparkling water of the canal across the street brushed past the swaying side-locks of the two tipsy fellows, who delighted in the refreshing coolness of the breeze and were far from being dampened by the autumn chill. The fair fellow in particular, had his chest so exposed as to reveal a cold-looking silver-chain hanging from his neck as an amulet.

They seemed to have wound up the lengthy talk which they had been holding, keeping even the maid at a discreet distance.

"So I've come back to Edo after three years'

---

[2] At a drinking bout, the Japanese, by way of making a show of their friendship, observe the custom of exchanging their cups with close friends.

absence," said the stout, swarthy man, unceremoni-
ously handing back his cup to the other, and
casually taking out his tobacco-case from under his
knee.

"Oh, now I understand why you've been so long
coming back. But now you're back and all Edo
folks will be happy, to say nothing of your own
henchmen."

"It's only you who say so."

"Ha, you don't mean that," answered the short
fair-complexioned fellow with a perverse grin,
glancing at the other with a feigned glare. "Ask the
landlady here, and you'll see."

"Hm, well," the man with a silver pipe in his
mouth, addressed as "Boss," gave a faint, grim
smile, but soon broke into a serious tone. "But
Edo, I imagine, has changed a lot in the three years
I was away."

"Yah, beyond all words. The gay quarters have
been shunned like a plague."

"Now things've come to such a head, old folks
often sigh for the good old days."

"It's only I who haven't changed. I've always
been poor." The fellow in the unlined kimono
with its finely checkered design laughingly gulped
the rice-wine in the cup which he had received
from his boss, and wiping a drop on the corner
of his mouth, raised his eyebrows as if to humble

himself. "Compared with the present, the world three years ago was a paradise on earth. Formerly, among robbers there were some fellows of consequence who carried a bit of weight like Nezumi-Kozo, even if he wasn't as good a robber as Ishikawa [3] Goemon."

"You talk mighty wild." The man in the old-style cloak said, choking with his own tobacco smoke, a sardonic smile playing on his countenance in spite of himself. "Who should ever treat robbers and me in the same light?"

"But you see," his audacious companion retorted, unconcerned by the remonstrance and swiggering another cup of rice-wine, to which he had helped himself. "In these days you'll find unscrupulous fellows who make money at every turn. But you never hear of an outstanding robber like him, do you?"

"You'd better not. Better there were no robbers in the country or mice in the house. Far better there were no notorious robbers."

"Of course, better none. Sure enough, better none," the fair-complexioned fellow said, stretching out his tattooed arm to fill his boss's cup with rice-wine and continued with a laugh. "Remembering those old days, strangely enough, I admire even

[3] A notorious robber, who was boiled to death in a caldron with his little son toward the end of the sixteenth century.

robbers. As you recall, Boss, that robber fellow, Nezumi-Kozo, sure had a mighty kindly and capital nature."

"Sure enough," his boss replied. "Gamblers are the ideal fellows to back up robbers."

"Ha, ha! You've got me there," he said, shrugging his shoulders. But in a second he went on in a cheerful voice. "They say he made a practice of breaking into the mansions of wealthy feudal lords to steal money from their safes and to give it in alms to the poor and needy. Good and evil are poles apart. But if I ever steal, I'd like to do this kind of good to bless my evil acts."

"I see. That sounds reasonable. I'm sure that Nezumi-Kozo, the robber, little dreams he's in your good graces, Handakamatsu. It might be good luck for him," the stout dark-complexioned man said to his companion in an extraordinarily quiet tone, returning his cup. But looking as if he had hit upon an idea, he tapped his knee and resumed his train of thought, a smile stealing over his countenance. "Now listen, with regard to Nezumi-Kozo, I was a party to a mighty ridiculous farce. Even now I never recall it without convulsing with laughter."

With this preface, the man addressed as "Boss" leisurely holding his pipe in his mouth, began to tell the following story, the smoke of his glowing tobacco curling lazily in the fading light of the setting sun.

* * * * * * *

It was just three years ago that out of my cussedness over the affair of the gambling house, I took off from Edo.

For a certain reason at the time, I did not dare to take the Tokaido Road, so I made my journey down the Koshu Road as far as Minobe, eighty miles west of Edo. If I remember correctly, it was on December the eleventh that, disguised as a traveler, I set out upon my journey from my quarters in Yotsuya, Edo.

I was clad in a lined pongee kimono that you may remember, fastened with a silken sash and wore a brown oilpaper raincoat and a sedge hat. Imagine how I felt traveling with no companion or burden other than a willow basket carried on my back. My steps might presumably have seemed buoyant and gay in my light outfit, with leggings and straw sandals on my feet. However, the thought of my being unable for the time being to set foot again on the soil of the capital so depressed my mind that, with each step I took, as the old-fashioned expression goes, my heart sank deeper into my boots.

On that day, as ill-luck would have it, under the lowering sky pregnant with snow, a biting wind was blowing across the plain, chilling me to the marrow. Far west of the Koshu Road along which I was plodding, towered the long range of be-clouded mountains way beyond the broad fields of mulberry trees, with not a dead leaf left to rustle in the gust of the freezing wind. A crow, clutching for dear life to a bare branch, appeared to have gotten his throat so sore because of the bitter cold that it could not even caw. From time to time sharp blasts of wind from Mt. Kobotoke, cavorting down upon the fields, would beat upon my flimsy raincoat and swirl it up, leaving me shivering and exposed to the relentless elements. I was unaccustomed to travel, and proud son of Edo that I was, found myself completely at the mercy of the miserable weather. After setting out from Yotsuya and even after passing Shinjuku on the lonely outskirts, I can't tell how often I looked back with longing eyes toward the Edo I had just left that morning on my westward journey.

My miserable appearance and lack of travel experience must have aroused the sympathy of onlookers. As I was passing by an inn in Fuchu, an honest-looking young fellow overtook me and engaged me in endless conversation.

I saw that he was wearing a dark blue raincoat and a sedge hat: the usual outfit of a traveler. But a discolored bundle hanging from his neck, gathered together by a faded cotton belt, a bald patch on his right temple, and his unshapely gaunt cheeks, all suggested that he was decidedly poverty-stricken and weather-beaten. But mind you, his affable glib tongue produced upon me the favorable impression that he was more kindly than he looked. He was thoughtful enough to point out to me the important sights and historical ruins on the way. At no other time in my life did I find myself more thankful for a traveling companion.

"Where are you going?" I asked.

"I'm going to Kofu. And you, sir?" he asked me in reply.

"I'm on my way to visit Minobe."

"You come from Edo, I'd guess. What part do you live in, sir?"

"Why, Kayabacho. Do you come from Edo, too?" I felt a quickened interest.

"Yes, I come from Fukagawa. I'm Echigoya Jukichi by name, and I'm a mere grocer by trade," he answered.

Briskly talking in such a nostalgic vein about our beloved Edo, we continued on our journey, each of us thinking that he had acquired a good companion.

Hurrying on our way, we were nearing the stage of Hino when soft snow flakes began to flutter down from the darkening sky. It was past four. Suppose that, traveling alone down there, you had looked up into the snowy sky and heard the plaintive notes of plovers hovering over the Tama River near by, you would have felt a chill creeping down your spine. Surely enough, you would have wanted to stop at Hino for the night. On that occasion, although he carried a lean purse, my companion, Echigoya Jukichi, was somebody for whom I could not but feel thankful.

"Sir," he said, "since it's snowing like this, I'm afraid we won't be able to make good progress at all tomorrow. So I think it would be better to go right on with our journey as far as Hachioji today."

At his suggestion, we pushed on our way through the snow to Hachioji, which greeted our eyes with a veritable snow-scene of a *ukiyoe* (color print). The white snow-laden roofs on both sides of the street were silhouetted in the dark which had already enveloped the streets. Here and there beneath the snow-laden roofs gently swayed illuminated red-paper lanterns amidst the clear tinkling of the approaching bells of belated horses.

"May I have the pleasure of your company tonight?" Echigoya Jukichi, stepping ahead of me in the snow, persistenly asked me.

"The pleasure is mine. I'll be glad to have a jolly time with you," I said since I had no objection. "Unfortunately I'm a stranger, and I don't know any inn here."

"Why, the one over there called 'the Yamajin'

is my favorite." As he said this, he showed me into the inn lit by hanging paper lanterns.

It was to all appearances a new establishment with a broad entrance and with the back directly connected to the kitchen. The clerk who had attached himself to the charcoal brazier by the counter hardly had time to order the maid to bring us a pail of water with which to wash our feet when, greedy as I might seem, the tantalizing odor of boiling rice and simmering soup mingling with clouds of steam greeted my nose. Hurriedly we took off our straw sandals, and led by the maid carrying a paper lantern, we went up the stairs into the upper room.

After taking a refreshing warm bath to banish our fatigue, we gulped down a few cups of hot rice-wine to shake off the cold, while Echigoya Jukichi, losing all control, began to make merry.

"Sir, you find the rice-wine to your taste, don't you?" The naturally glib-tongued fellow prattled on aimlessly. "Go up the Koshu Road from here, and you'll never be able to get rice-wine like this." He laughed. "Let me sing an old song. 'I'm a yoeman's wife. I've been oft . . .'"

That was not so bad. When we had drained two or three bottles of rice-wine, he started singing in a trembling voice, with the corners of his eyes narrowed down, shaking his scooped chin and twitching his nose:

"Wine is my foe!
—On its ruinous way,
With one drink only,
Aha! 'Twas a wench led me astray."

I didn't know what to do with him, and I thought there was no alternative but to put him to bed. So, taking an opportune moment, I ordered dinner served.

"We're leaving quite early tomorrow morning, so we'd better go to bed now." I managed to hurry him into bed, although he still had a lingering thirst for drink.

He should have thanked heaven. The minute he laid his head on the pillow, the fellow who had been so merry and sportive gave an alcoholic yawn and once more wailed in an uncanny voice, "Aha! 'Twas a wench led me astray." Presently his screech passed into snores, and for all the noisy scampering of rats, he was too fast asleep to toss even in the least in his bed.

But I was in bad luck. You see, that was my first night's stop on my journey from Edo. My companion's snores jarred on my ears. Strangely enough, the more hushed the surroundings became, the harder I found it to go to sleep. Outside it didn't seem to have stopped snowing. I imagined that at times I heard the sound of the snow against the shutters. The rogue asleep in bed close by me might easily be humming some jolly melody in his dream. But in Edo there might be a dear one or two spending a sleepless night worrying over me— this kept me wide-awake for quite a long while and I was anxiously hoping for the dawn. Thus I heard the wall clock strike at twelve, and again at two in the morning. But it seemed that in the course of time I had dropped off into drowsiness. By and by I awoke to find the flickering light from the paper lantern was out; it might have been snuffed out by a rat. On top of that, the fellow that had been snoring so loudly a little while ago was as still as death, and even his breathing could not be heard. I hardly had time to wonder what could be the matter when a hand stealthily groped its way into my bed. Trembling nervously, it searched for the knot of my money belt. Appearances are deceptive, indeed. The rogue was a thief. But a thief should be of better mettle. This thought nearly provoked my laughter. But it was exasperating to think that I had been drinking with the thief until just a little time ago. So the instant his hand began untying the knot of my money belt, I grabbed his hand and wrenched it. He was struck by surprise and while he was struggling to free himself, I smothered him in a quilt, head and all. The bastard wriggled and struggled, and on thrusting his head out from under the quilt with difficulty, he gave an odd, queer scream, "Mur-, mur-, murder," as a hen would do if she tried to crow! If the thief himself called for help, he would spare me the trouble. I had known him for a scoundrel since the time I met him. But this act of unmanly dishonesty was enough to enrage me, and seizing a wooden pillow hard by, I gave him a few whacks across his face.

Aroused by the melée, the guests close by, the landlord, and the servants rushed headlong upstairs, with lighted candles in their hands, wondering what could have happened, and they saw the scoundrel lying flat under my thighs, gasping for breath, with only his funny-looking face thrust out of the quilt. Everybody burst into hilarious laughter.

"Hey, landlord," I said. "I've got a damned flea pestering me. Sorry for alarming you. Offer my humble apology to all the guests, please."

That was all I had to say. I didn't have to tell them the particulars. The servants among them bound the captive tightly hand and foot, and dragged him downstairs as though they had just caught a monster alive.

"I'm really sorry you've met with such an unexpected misfortune," the landlord apologized after coming up to me immediately to beg my forgiveness, with repeated subservient bows. "What a great surprise it must have been to you! But it's a great relief that you haven't had anything stolen,

[110]

including your traveling money. Later, as soon as day dawns, the rogue shall be handed over to the public office, so I beg of you a thousand pardons for being remiss in our service and for our failure to take necessary precautions."

"Oh, the oversight was mine," I said. "I happened to fall into his company, little dreaming he was a thief. So there's no reason for you to beg my pardon. Here, take this small gratuity for the trouble I've given you. You might treat the young folks who were good to me, say, to a bowl of hot noodles."

He went downstairs, making a couple of bows because of the gratuity. When I was left alone, turning the matter over in my mind, I thought it would be stupid of me to lie in bed indefinitely as if I had been snubbed by a whore in a stage-town. Before long it would be six o'clock. I concluded I could do nothing better than to make an early start right away, although the road was still dark.

After making up my mind, I got ready at once, and walked quietly to the top of the stairs so as not to disturb the other guests, with the idea of paying my bill at the counter. Then I heard several voices. All the servants still seemed to be up and busy. While wondering what they could be about, I heard the name, "Nezumi-Kozo," you mentioned a little while ago. I thought it very strange, and peered down from the top of the stairs, with my willow basket in my hand. Then I saw, in the middle of the large bare hall, the wretch, Echigoya Jukichi sitting cross-legged, with the end of the rope which bound him fast to the pillar. Around him in the light of the big candle there stood talking, three young men including the clerk, all with their sleeves tucked up.

"Sure, as this damned thief puts on years, he might make a robber more wicked than Nezumi-Kozo," the bald-headed clerk who had been fussing and fuming was heard blustering, with his hand firmly clutching an abacus. "If that should turn out to be the case, he'll bring discredit on all the inns on the highway. I guess it would do people a good service to kill him."

"That's ridiculous. How could this numbskull play the part of Nezumi-Kozo?" cut in a horse-driver in a workman's coat, staring fixedly at the thief. "You clerks ought to be capable of better judgment. Just look this rascal in the face, and you can tell if he's got guts."

"Sure," said the youngster of the inn, armed with a bamboo blower in his hand. "He can't be any better than a weasel cub at most."

"Really. This damned monkey of a fellow'll be robbed of everything he's got before he picks another's pocket."

"Instead of taking to the highway, he'd better

fish with children for farthings in shrine offertories, putting in his rod with its limed tip."

"No, he'd better remain standing in my buck millet field in place of a scarecrow."

While they were taunting him, he had been only blinking his eyes out of vexation for a few moments till the youngster of the inn put his bamboo blower under his chin to jerk up his head. This set his tongue blabbing in a torrent of vulgar language.

"Hey! Hey! Shut up, you damned rabble! Who do you think you're talking all this absurd nonsense about? I tell you that, such as I may seem, I'm a robber of some notoriety and have knocked about all over Japan. You should know what you are. You jackanapes! How dare you wretched servants spew out all this impudence?"

This amazed them all. I had been stepping downstairs, but astonished at his exhibition of bravado, I paused halfway to watch how the matter would turn out. Among them all, the clerk, who looked so evidently good-natured, stared hard at the unrepentant and indignant captive in such complete bewilderment that he had forgotten that he held an abacus in his hand. However, all the threatening outburst of the captive culprit fell flat on the horse-driver, who was stout-hearted.

"What good is there in a thief?" retorted the driver. "Don't you know that I was the horse-driver of the Yokohama Stage who caught a snarling wolf alive in that terrible thunder storm three years ago? Mind you, if I exert myself, I can kick a mere thief to death.

"I'll be hanged if I get scared by your downright threats," the thief said with derisive laughter. "Here I'll unveil my career, which will more than startle you out of your drowsiness. Now prick up your ears and listen to what I'll tell you."

He blustered into his awkward imitation of an actor's voice, while his face looked miserably cold with a dewdrop sparkling under his nose. Moreover, the ugly bruise across his face made by my heavy blow had swollen from the temple down to the chin. But his pompous, affected speech must have had some tangible effect on these country bumpkins. While, with contemptuous tosses of his head, he went on bragging loudly of his evil acts to which he had been apprenticed since his childhood, even the shaggy-bearded horse-driver, who boastfully claimed to have captured a snarling wolf alive, came to set himself against the scoundrel less defiantly. When the thief saw that his audience was becoming browbeaten under his devilish tongue, he fiercely glared at them and went on with his pompous speech.

"Pshaw! Damn you bastards!" the thief went on. "Did you think I'm such a milksop as to be scared of you? You're mistaken if you think you've an ordinary thief to deal with. I guess you remember well the burglar that stole into the squire's here at this very stage on that stormy night last fall and went off with all his money. He was no other than *me.*"

"You . . . into the squire's?" The clerk was not the only one that was startled. They all, even the driver that had the bamboo blower in his hand fell back a pace or two in open-mouthed amazement.

"Yah! Seeing you're astonished at such acts, you must be a bunch of weaklings," he bragged on. "Hey, listen! You know only a few days ago two couriers were murdered at the Kobotoke Pass. Now whose doing do you think it was?"

The villain, sniffing rudely, prattled on about one hideous crime after another that came into his head: intrepidly breaking into a warehouse in Fuchu, secretly setting fire to a house at the stage of Hino, and lustfully raping a woman pilgrim in the mountain off the Atsugi Road. As he went on blabbing out these sensational tales, the clerk and his boorish companions gradually assumed unconsciously a more courteous attitude toward the scoundrel. Above all, when I heard the driver groan, "What a real scoundrel you are!" folding his brawny arms over his massive chest, I was so overwhelmed with the ridiculousness of the situation that I very nearly burst out laughing.

The thief appeared exceedingly cold, with his teeth clattering helplessly, but his lips were spirited enough to blurt out, "Hey, gather up your scattered wits, all of you! I'm of a better mettle and character than you. To tell the truth, I ran off from Edo, as folks got wind of my strangling my own mother to death—you see, you each have only one mother—because I wanted to lay my hands on her pin money." At the confession of his heinous atrocity, they were all struck dumb with amazement, and looked into his face, that was quite painfully swollen from the temples to the chin, with as much admiration as though they would have looked up into the face of a talented star actor.

I thought it too stupid to stand as a gaping spectator any longer and went down a few steps when the bald-headed clerk, clapping his hands, abruptly cried out, "Now I see. Yes, I see. It's a sure thing! Nezumi-Kozo is your nickname, isn't it?" That changed my mind. And being anxious to hear what he would say next, I stopped halfway down the stairs.

"Since you guessed right, I suppose I have to confess now," the villain declared, glaring at the clerk with a scornful grin. "Indeed, Nezumi-Kozo whose name is ringing all over Edo is none other than *me*."

But he had hardly said so when a chilly shudder convulsed his whole frame, and a fit of violent sneezing shook him utterly to spoil the impression of fierceness in his glare. Nevertheless, the three fellows could not have led him on more enthusiastically than they might have done a champion wrestler who presented himself before a feverishly excited audience.

"Really, I thought as much," the driver said, as if impressed. "The Kanta of the Yokohama Stage who captured the wolf alive in the heavy rain three years ago—that was myself—my name is enough to hush a crying child. But even in my very presence you didn't seem to flinch at all."

"Sure, his eyes've got a sharp look about them."

"Really didn't I tell you that he'd make a notorious robber a notch above the average? For all that, you know, the best swimmer sometimes gets drowned, and there's many a slip between the cup and the lip, as the proverb goes. If he hadn't been caught, he'd have robbed all the guests upstairs of all their money."

Although they were unwilling to untie his bonds, they came to show him every courtesy. This made him swell with such overbearing pride that he dared to give peremptory orders to everyone.

"Hey, clerk. It's good luck for the inn of your master that you've put up Nezumi-Kozo. So don't bring bad luck to your inn by keeping my lips dry and parched. Now bring me a quart of rice-wine. I don't mind drinking it straight from the measure."

The scoundrel was impudent, indeed. But how stupid the clerk was naïvely to follow his orders! While I was watching the bald-headed clerk give the tipsy thief rice-wine to drink from a quart measure, I was overwhelmed with the ridiculous absurdity not only of the servants of the inn but of folks in the world at large. What do you say? Among those lumped together as scoundrels, filchers are lesser criminals than burglars, and pickpockets than incendiaries. So the world ought to be more lenient toward lesser than toward greater thieves. But that's not the case with man. He's often harsh with a petty gambler but is liable to bow to a notorious scoundrel. He will give Nezumi-Kozo a drink, but beat down a common thief. If I were a thief, I'd not like to be just a pilferer, I thought. But I couldn't remain indefinitely an idle onlooker of such a farce. So with deliberate steps I went downstairs.

"Hey, clerk," I called, flinging my things down at his feet. "I'm leaving very early, so make out my bill, please." Thrown into helpless shame-faced confusion and utter embarrassment, the clerk quickly handed the measure to the driver, and repeatedly putting his hand upon his temple, he sputtered incoherently. "Oh, I hope you're not offended, sir. . . . Thank you very much for giving us a gratuity a little while ago . . . I'm glad it's stopped snowing."

"Just as I came down, I heard this thieving fellow is the notorious Nezumi-Kozo. Is that true?" I asked the clerk, quite amused by his awkward effort to cover his confusion.

"Yes, sir, so he is, I'm told," he stammered out his answer. "Hey, bring this gentleman's straw sandals quick. Oh, I see. Here's your sedge hat and oilpaper overcoat. He's a damn thief, isn't he? . . . Yes, I'll make out your bill right away, sir."

Scolding the youngster to cover his own awkward position, with his fingers he began flicking his abacus, his writing-brush in his mouth, as if to work out a total.

In the meantime I put on my straw sandals, and prepared to smoke my pipe.

The thief looked quite tipsy already, with his face flushed even to the bald patch at his temples. However, he mightn't have been quite dead to shame. He was turned aside so he would not be able to see me. At the sight of his wretched plight, I was somewhat moved to pity him.

"Hey, Ichigoya-san. I say, Jukichi-san. You'd better not play silly jokes." I talked to him kindly. "If you insist on being Nezumi-Kozo, simple good-natured country folks will swallow your story. That'll do you no good, I'm afraid."

"What? Do you mean to say I'm not Nezumi-

Kozo?" The rascally crook didn't mind acting another scene. "Hm, you've got a good stock of information, indeed. As we can see, sir, you're quite a bit stuck-up."

"Come, come. If you want to brag, the driver and youngsters here would be your good companions for your swaggering. But as they've been listening all this time, I guess they've got tired." I went on reasoning with him. "First of all, if you were undoubtedly the greatest robber in Japan, you'd be the last one to prattle about your old crimes. What good would that do you? Come, now. Listen to me, will you? If you're obstinate enough to say you're Nezumi-Kozo, the officials and all the folks around may think you're really Nezumi-Kozo. Then your lightest punishment would bring you to the gallows, and your heaviest would nail you to the cross. Still will you insist you're Nezumi-Kozo when you are questioned?"

"I don't know how to apologize," the bastard answered, turning pale in an instant. "Really I'm not Nezumi-Kozo. I'm a mere thief."

"Yes, you must be." Assuming a serious look, I made fun of him, knocking out the ashes from my pipe. "But since you say you've set fire to and have broken into so many houses, you must be a good bit of a scoundrel. Anyway you'll have to go to the gallows."

"No, sir, they're all lies." The sniveling thief,

who had already sobered up, said in a tearful voice. "As I told you, I'm a grocer by trade named Echigoya Jukichi. I travel up and down this road once or twice a year, and naturally I have a good stock of all sorts of rumors and hearsay good and bad. So I've been prattling anything and everything irresponsible that came into my head."

"Listen here. You've just said you're a mere thief. In all my days, I've never heard of a thief peddling groceries."

"Honest to God! This is the first time in my life that I've ever laid my hands on another's property. This fall my wife left me. Ever since then I've had a series of mishaps. Poverty dulls the wit, you know, and on the impulse of the moment, I committed this outrageous breach of etiquette."

However stupid, I was well aware that he was a disguised thief. So amazed at his random quibbling, I remained silent as I filled my pipe with tobacco. I was simply amazed. But the driver and the youngsters were more than infuriated. Before I had time to stop them, they knocked him down.

"How dare you try to make a fool of us?"

"We'll knock you down," they cried in a determined chorus.

At their savage yells, the bamboo blower and the measure fell upon him, and their sharp blows and violent kicks rained down on him mercilessly.

Poor Echigoya Jukichi's face was badly bruised and his head swollen with lumps.

*　　*　　*　　*　　*　　*　　*

"This is all of the story," he said. The stout dark-complexioned man, who had told the particulars of the story, took up the cup which had lain neglected on the table.

The sun no longer shone upon the white walls of the canal, and the shades of evening were closing in around the willow tree across the canal. Just at this time the curfew of the Jozoji Temple on the hill nearby tolled into the hearts of the two talkers the chill of the coming fall, vibrating the quiet air beyond the balustrade redolent of the faint tang of the sea. The rattan blind waving in the breeze, the cawing of crows in the Ohama Palace, and the cold sparkling water in the cup basin in front of them—it could not be long before the red flickering light of a candle stand would be brought upstairs by the maid.

"By jove! What a damned scoundrel he was!" The fellow wearing the unlined fine checkered kimono exclaimed, putting his hand to the bottom of the rice-wine bottle the second he saw his boss had emptied his cup. "What the hell did he think of my favorite patron god of Japanese robbers, Nezumi-Kozo? Setting you, my own boss, aside, if I'd been in your place, I'd sure have knocked the damned fool down."

"Nezumi-Kozo may be happy to think that even such a lout could lord it over others simply because he called himself Nezumi-Kozo."

"But to think such a cub thief should've called himself Nezumi-Kozo...." The short tattooed fellow looked as if he had wished to make some further remonstrance.

"Hm, I've kept this from you till now," the dark-complexioned man in the old-style cloak said, with a leisurely smile playing around his lips.

"This is dead sure, as I myself tell you," he continued with his cup in his mouth, glancing about with watchful eyes. "Even as I am both Izumiya Jirokichi and Nezumi-Kozo who was on everybody's tongue in Edo three years ago, really are one and the same."

HEICHU, THE AMOROUS GENIUS

Heichu was famous as a great lover. There was not a lady at court or a girl of humble birth that was not eager to steal a look at him.

Gleanings from Uji (Uji Shui Monogatari) [1]

Heichu so longed to see the woman of his heart that he finally fell ill and pined away out of love to the day of his death.

Tales Old and New (Konjaku Monogatari) [2]

Such is the path which the amorous tread.

The Ten Edifications (Jukkunsho) [3]

1. A PICTURE OF HEICHU

Wearing an elegant and graceful head-gear, a symbol of the peaceful age, an exceedingly hand-

[1] Uji Shui Monogatari is a collection of tales compiled during the 13th century.

[2] Konjaku Monogatari is a collection of tales and episodes compiled during the 12th century. Many of Akutagawa's stories are based on these two collections.

[3] Jukkunsho is a 13th century collection of philosophic writings.

some and fair-complexioned man is facing us. The hairs of his mustache under his shapely nose are as pronounced as though they were painted in thin India ink. Amiable smiles radiate from his rather narrow eyes, so crystal clear that they appear as if they had caught the bright glow of full-blown cherry-blossoms.

However, a closer look may bring to light the sober truth that complete happiness does not always dwell therein. For his smiles seem to yearn after something far away and to frown upon everything nearby.

What appears obscurely behind him may be either a screen on which cranes are woven or a sliding screen (*shoji*) which shows a red pine growing at the foot of a mountain.

That is the colorful image of Tairano Sadamori, "the greatest of all lovers," or our Japanese Don Juan, as he appears to me from my reading the stories about him in the old tales. His father, Tairano Yoshikage, had three sons, of whom he was the second. So he is said to have been nicknamed Heichu.[4]

---

[4] "Hei" is the Chinese reading of the same Chinese ideograph, of which the Japanese reading is "Taira" (flat). "Chu" is another Chinese ideograph meaning middle.

2. THE CHERRY-BLOSSOMS

Heichu, leaning on the pillar, gazed idly at the cherry-blossoms in his garden. The blossoms on the branches spreading out close to the eaves, seemed to be a little past their full glory. The long-afternoon sunlight reflected their delicate shadows causing them to lose some of their bright pink, upon their interlaced sprigs. His eyes were fixed upon the blossoms, but his heart was far away. He had been thinking about the lady's maid of his heart.

"I wonder when I met her for the first time," he thought to himself. "As I heard that she was going to visit the festival Harvest Shrine, it must have been on the morning of the first of February. She was about to get into her carriage when I happened to pass by. Yes, that was the first time I met her. I caught only a glimpse of her face which she was shading with her fan. She was dressed in a plum-blossom-red silk kimono over a bright green undergarment, covered by a purple-colored outer garment. Her attractive costume added to her charm beyond words. As she was getting into her carriage, plucking up her skirt with one hand, she gracefully bowed. Her fascination at that time was irresistible. Among the many ladies in the Premier's palace, she was a peerless beauty.

It's no wonder then, that I should fall in love with her . . .

"But am I really in love with her?" he continued to think, looking serious. "I seem to be in love with her, and I don't. The more I think about this affair, the harder it becomes for me to decide. Yet I have to admit I am in love with her. However dearly I may love her, I am not blinded by love. Once when I talked about her with Norizane, a courtier, he made the priggish remark that it was a pity she had thin hair. I noticed it at once. Norizane may be something of a piper, but in a discourse about a love affair . . . Well, let him be. For the present I want to think only about her. I'd say that her face looks a little too lonely. A lonely face ought to have something elegant about it, like an old picture on a scroll. Hers has some queer composure which calls for caution. I shouldn't be surprised if a woman who looks like her should make a fool of a man. Nor can you say that she has a fair complexion. Although not dark, she is some-what amber-complexioned. I can never look at her without being captivated by her irresistible charm. In feminine charm, she is beyond all comparison.

"I've sent her ever so many letters, but she hasn't sent me a single reply. I've never had such an obsti-nate girl to deal with." Knees drawn up, Heichu pensively looked up beyond the eaves into the sky, and he saw the pale blue sky checkered with clusters of cherry-blossoms. "Most women yield to my wishes the third time I write to them. I've never had to write more than five times to a woman of the strictest chastity. One poem of mine was sufficient to win the heart of the daughter of a celebrated sculptor of Buddhist statues, Egen. And it wasn't a poem of my own composition. Oh, yes, it was Yoshisuke's work. I hear he sent the poem to his love, a low-ranking court-lady, but she would take no notice of his attentions. Even if the poem were the same, if I were to send it, ... The lady's maid, however, hasn't written to me, although I sent her my poems. So perhaps I can't be very proud. But anyway all my letters are sure to get answers from women. If I get answers, we meet and I'm made much of, after which I soon get bored. That's the fixed routine of my love affairs. I've already written her as many as twenty letters with no success. I don't carry an inexhaustible stock of love-letter styles and mine is nearly at an end. In my letter that I sent her today, I wrote, 'Kindly condescend to indulge me with at least two words, "I looked." ' So I expect this time I shall hear from her—but I wonder if any answer will come. If it doesn't ... Ah, me! Till some time ago I wasn't so weak-kneed as to worry so much over this kind of thing. They say the old fox at the Buraku Palace assumes the shape of a woman. Those bewitched by such a fox must feel something like this.

"She really wears out my patience." With his eyes turned toward the sky, Heichu quietly stifled a yawn. From time to time above the eaves, the flashes of white wings were seen flitting in the declining sunlight. The cooing of pigeons came from somewhere. "Even if she doesn't consent to have a rendezvous, once I talk to her, I'm sure I'll win her heart. Until the court ladies, Settsu and Kochujo, knew me, they were men-haters. Once they fell into my hands, they became so amorous. This woman is not stone or wood. I don't see why I shouldn't win her heart. I don't think that at the last moment she will behave as shyly as Kochujo did. Neither will she act with queer indifference as Settsu did. She'll put her sleeve to her mouth, and with smiles in her eyes, she . . ."

"My lord!" a voice was heard.

"Anyway it will be at night," his imagination went on. "A rush light is burning. The light will fall on her hair . . ."

"My lord!" the voice repeated.

Heichu, a little confused, turned his head with his soft headgear on, and found that, before he was aware of it, his page with eyes cast down had been holding out a letter. Surely enough, he must have been doing his best to stifle a laugh.

"A letter?"

"Yes, from the lady's maid, my lord." So saying, the page hurriedly retired.

"From the lady's maid? Really, I wonder?" Heichu nervously opened the letter written on a sheet of thin blue-colored paper. "Maybe this is a prank played by Norizane or Yoshisuke. They're all leisured men who are more fond of this kind of mischief than of anything else. Oh, my! This is *her* letter. Certainly this is *her* handwriting. What does it say? Well, what does this sentence mean?"

The instant he read the letter, he threw it away. For in answer to his letter saying, "Kindly condescend to indulge me with at least two words, 'I looked,'" he found just the two words, "I looked" in her letter, and that the very two words that he wrote had been cut out from his own letter and pasted on a blank sheet of paper.

"To think that I, Heichu, reputed to be the greatest of all lovers should be made fun of like this! What a disgrace! What a pert girl the lady's maid is! You'll see what I'll do to her . . ." Holding his knees with his hands, Heichu stupidly looked up at the top of the cherry-blossoms. The petals of the blossoms fell like so many dancing snow-flakes from above the sprouting young green leaves waving in the wind.

3. THE RAINY NIGHT

It was about two months later. One night during a long steady rainfall, Heichu attempted a stealthy visit to the apartment of the lady's maid. The rain was falling with such a terrific force as if the night sky would melt. The roads were flooded and muddy in many places. "Since I'm taking all this trouble going out to meet her tonight in this terrible rainstorm, the most heartless lady's maid will be touched with compassion," he thought to himself on the way.

Arriving at the door, Heichu gave a tap with his silver-gilt folding-fan and cleared his throat before asking for admission. Then a fifteen year old girl came out immediately. The hour being late, her painted precocious-looking face looked sleepy. He whispered asking her to announce his visit to the lady's maid.

The girl withdrew, and coming back to the door, she also answered in a low voice, "Come in this way, please, and wait a while. Everyone will retire presently. She says she will be pleased to meet you then."

Heichu smiled in spite of himself. When he was shown in, he sat down by the side of the sliding-door of the room which seemed to adjoin that of the lady's maid.

"I'm resourceful," he said to himself with a smile

after the girl withdrew. "Proud as she is, the lady's maid seems to have given in at last. Woman is susceptible to tender pathos. Show her kindnesses, and she will fall a ready prey to you. Neither Yoshisuke nor Norizane have this knack, but after all they . . .

"But let me see. . . . It seems too good to be true that I am to meet her." Kept waiting alone in the dark, Heichu began to feel uneasy. "It's unlikely that the woman who has kept on refusing me so provokingly should consent to meet me. I've written her about sixty letters and she hasn't sent me a single reply. So why shouldn't I be doubtful of her sincerity? Anyway could it be possible that the lady's maid who has so obstinately refused to take any notice of me, should ever . . . ? Carefully considering it, I feel sure my doubts are not wholly unfounded. For all that, she may possibly have been overcome by my persistent courtship. At any rate it's I, Heichu, who has been making love to her. Moved by my earnest plea, her heart might have suddenly melted. Fortune will often take an ironic turn. So the best thing I can do is to think that my doubt is wrong. Then the girl will presently . . .

"Now it is most important for me to be patient." Straightening his kimono, he looked around nervously. But he could see nothing but darkness. At that moment the pelting of the rain on the shingled roof became louder and the sounds pervaded the room. He picked up his attentive ears, as the bustle and shuffle of the passers-by came from the corridor. To the monotonous accompaniment of the ceaseless pattering of the rain, the Court ladies who had been serving in the Premier's presence were probably returning to their respective apartments.

"In about half an hour I'll be able to gratify my long-cherished desire to the full," his thoughts continued. "But I can't be quite sure yet. Well, I'll give up thinking about meeting her, and strangely enough, I'll be able to meet her. But ironical fortune may have seen through my innermost design. So I'll think about meeting her. For all that, things may not turn out according to my calculations . . . Ah, my heart pains me. I'd rather think of things that have nothing to do with her. All that I can hear is the sound of the rain. Now I'll close my eyes and think about it. How many phrases are there with rain in them, I wonder?—raindrops, raincoats, rainbows . . ."

He had been turning over such thoughts in his mind, when to his great surprise, he heard an unexpected sound. It might have been more accurate to say that the sound came like the announcement of the advent of Buddha to his believers. His face brimmed over with greater ecstasy than ever did that of a devout priest. For he distinctly heard someone unfastening the latch of the sliding-door on the other side of the room. The door opened and slid on the sill. Simultaneously a sweet aroma wafted into the room which was completely dark. He knelt down and groped his way slowly on his knees in the intriguing darkness. There was not a sound to be heard but for the persistent pattering of the rain on the roof, nor a single sign to be seen. What his hand touched here and there proved to be the clothes-hanger and the mirror-stand. He felt his heart thumping faster and more heavily.

"Is she here? If she is, she'll certainly say something." Then his hand happened to feel the soft hand of the woman. He continued feeling around with his hand, and it touched her sleeve which felt like silk. After that it reached her breast under her kimono, her soft neck and full cheek, and then her comparatively icy-cold hair. He had at last fumbled his way to the lady's maid of his heart lying close in front of him. Kissing her hand with his trembling lips, he, too, lay down.

This was no dream or vision. *His* dear woman, who lay disheveled close to him, wearing only a thin silk outer garment, was an irresistible magnet for him. Trembling all over he drew closer to her. But she remained perfectly still without stirring an inch. He remembered reading about something like this in an old storybook. He might possibly have seen something similar in the picture-scroll which years ago he had unrolled in the light of a large rush-lantern in the Imperial Palace.

"How grateful I am to you! I thought till now that you were unkind and unfeeling to me. But from now on I'll devote myself to you rather than to Buddha," drawing her closer to him, he wished to whisper in her ear. But however eagerly he tried to speak, his voice was choked up and his tongue stuck to his palate. In the meantime, the delicate scent of her hair and the strangely warm and delightful fragrance of her soft skin unreservedly enveloped him. At this instant her breath wafted over his face.

An instant—this instant over, and amidst the passing storm of their amorous passion, they would have become oblivious to the sound of the rain, the aromatic perfume, the Premier in the Palace, and the court ladies.

At this very instant, the lady's maid raised herself, and bringing her face close to his, said shyly, "Wait a minute, please. The door over there isn't latched yet. Let me go and latch it."

Heichu nodded. She tip-toed off, leaving her sweet, delicate scent behind. With his eyes wide open, he lay impatiently waiting for her return. After a while he heard a gentle sliding of the door and the clicking of the closing latch.

[135]

Then he was reminded of an old poem.

> Things you think are true
> In dark of night,
> And dreams vain and vivid
> Are in substance *one*.

After some time he raised himself. The air was as fragrant as before. But nothing was to be seen but the darkness. His dear lady had gone somewhere, and even the rustling of her clothes was not to be heard.

"Surely not! But she may possibly..." he thought. Getting up, he fumbled his way again, and he reached the door. There he found that the door was latched on the outside. He listened, but he could not hear a single footstep. All the apartments of the court ladies were deep in silence.

"Heichu, Heichu, you're no longer the greatest lover under the sun." Stupefied with despair, he mumbled, leaning on the door. "Your personal charm had faded. Neither is your gift as remarkable as before. You're a more contemptible wretch than Norizane and Yoshisuke."

4. HEICHU LAMENTS

One day feeling helpless and forlorn, Heichu stood in the deserted corridor near the lady's maid's apartment not far from the Premier's hall. The

oily luster of the sunlight falling on the balustrade
was a fair indication that the day would bring swel-
tering heat. Beyond the eaves, the luxuriant ver-
dure of a clump of pine trees afforded a quiet coolness in the heat.

"The lady's maid determinedly rejects my approaches. I've given her up." Looking pale, he
thought seriously. "But however hard I try to get
her out of my mind, her enthralling figure haunts
my eyes. To dispel her from my thoughts, how
often I have offered my earnest prayers to the gods
of all quarters! And yet I could not go to the
Kamo [5] Shrine without clearly perceiving her face
in the enshrined mirror. Nor could I visit the inner
hall of the Kiyomizu Temple [5] without seeing the
statue of the Goddess of Mercy turn into that of
the lady's maid.

"There is only one way left for me to forget her.
That is to find something repulsive in her," he continued to think. "The lady's maid is no celestial
being, so she may have some impurities within her.
If I can ever see just one of them, my enthralling
vision of her will vanish, as does that of Reynard
the fox (which has assumed the form of one's wife)
the moment its cloven hoof is unmasked. Not until
then will my life be really mine. Hail to the Goddess of Great Mercy and Compassion, reveal to me

[5] Both the Kamo Shrine and the Kiyomizu Temple are among
the noted sights of historical interest in the city of Kyoto.

the sobering proof that the lady's maid is not really in substance different from a beggar woman on the street." So thinking, he cast upwards a languid look.

"Oh, there comes the girl attendant of the apartment of the lady's maid."

The bright-looking girl happened to come toward him, wearing a pink-colored garment and a dark crimson skirt. She was hiding something like a small casket behind her red fan which she had spread over it. He thought that she must be going to throw away the lady's maid's waste matter. At the sight of her a bold determination suddenly flashed through his mind like lightning. With a fierce glare in his eyes, he barred her way, and as soon as he snatched up the casket from her hands, he sped away with it into a vacant room. The girl taken by surprise, ran after him, pit-a-pat, raising wild outcries. But Heichu had no sooner plunged into the room than he quickly fastened the latch of the door.

"Yes, if I look inside this, one's hundred-year-old love will vanish like a vain dream." With his trembling hand, he held it up. The casket was of new exquisite workmanship with gold lacquer design.

"Her waste matter is in here, and my life, too," he said and stood gazing intently at the beautiful casket. The girl's tearful outcries continued outside, but in the course of time subsided into silence.

He was now in such nervous excitement that both the door and the paper sliding-screen (*shoji*) began to fade away like mists before his eyes, and he became incapable of discerning night from day. Only the casket with the gold-lacquered cuckoo in relief on it, loomed up distinctly before his eyes. "To forget her and to live on, both depend on this casket. If I only open this lid, all my . . . Well, no! This is the point I have to think over." He hesitated at the last moment, traces of tears glistening on his cheeks. "I can't make up my mind which to do. To forget her and live an insignificant life or to die with my memory of her captivating beauty. Even if I die, shall I leave this lid unopened?"

After meditating for a short while, in his mind he cried out hysterically, his eyes flashing. "Heichu, Heichu! What a coward you are! Have you forgotten that rainy night? She may be still mocking at your love now. Live on! Brace up! and live on! Look at her waste matter, and you'll be sure to triumph over her."

At last frantically he took off the lid. He saw the inside half-full of light orange-colored water with two or three dark orange-colored stick-like substances down on the bottom. At the same time the perfume of clove tickled his nose as if he were in a dream. Could this be her waste matter? Neither Venus nor Aphrodite would have such waste matter. Knitting his brow, he picked up a substance about two inches long floating uppermost, putting it close to his nose again and again. It was doubtless the odor of extra fine aloes wood.

"How's this? Her water seems to be fragrant, too. Maybe this is perfume, too." Cocking his head, he softly sipped the water. Undoubtedly it was clear liquid obtained by boiling down clove wood.

He chewed and tasted the substance he had picked. It had such a mixture of sweet and bitter tastes and his mouth immediately became saturated with a perfume stronger and more delicate than the fragrance of mandarin-orange blossoms. The lady's maid somehow had seen through what Heichu had in view, and to frustrate his design, she had made elaborate waste matter out of fragrant wood.

"Lady's maid, you've killed Heichu," he groaned and cast down the gold-lacquered casket. Then he fell flat on the floor. In his eyes, the lady's maid of enthralling beauty, with her head surmounted by an aureole, was smiling at him.

5. NOTE ON THE STORY

Here is a part of the gossip between two friends of Heichu's, Yoshisuke and Norizane.

Yoshisuke: They say even Heichu is no match for the lady's maid.

Norizane: Yes, so they say.

Yoshisuke: He will make advances to any woman

except the court ladies in Imperial attendance and of the Imperial Wardrobe. That should be a good lesson to him.

Norizane: Are you a follower of Confucius, too?

Yoshisuke: I don't know anything about Confucius' teachings. But I know full well that so many women have been brought to grief at Heichu's hand. And I'm well aware of the terrible sufferings their husbands had to bear, the bitter grief that parents had to endure, and the deep grudge their relatives had to nurse. Those who cause such trouble should be subject to public censure.

Norizane: But that isn't always the case. Really Heichu may be causing trouble to the public, but I'd say he alone shouldn't be held responsible.

Yoshisuke: Then who else should?

Norizane: The women should.

Yoshisuke: It's wrong for the women to be held responsible for the guilt.

Norizane: I'd say it isn't fair for only Heichu to be held responsible.

Yoshisuke: But he has made amorous approaches to so many women. Anyhow this much is certain: we don't cause trouble to people, like Heichu does.

Norizane: You can't be so sure about that. I don't know why, but being human, we can't live a minute without hurting one another. The only difference is that Heichu gives more trouble than we. This is a fate unavoidable to a man of genius.

Yoshisuke: The carp in this pond might as well be dragons since Heichu might be classed with geniuses.

Norizane: Undoubtedly Heichu is a genius. Notice his attractive face. Listen to his suave voice. Read his excellent letters. If you were a woman, I bet you would fall in love with him. From the moment he left his mother's womb, he was endowed with extraordinary gifts as was Saint Kukai [6] and Onono Dofu.[7] If he were not a genius, there would be no geniuses in the world. In sheer genius we can in no way measure up to him.

Yoshisuke: Geniuses may commit sins, but they do a lot of good. For instance, see Onono Dofu's calligraphy, and you'll be moved by the wonderful strokes of the master brush. Listen to Saint Kukai chanting a prayer or a Buddhist sutra, and . . .

Norizane: I don't mean to say that geniuses do nothing but commit sins. I mean they commit sins as well.

Yoshisuke: Then they differ from Heichu who does nothing but commit sins.

Norizane: That's the point we are not qualified to judge. To those who cannot read even the Japanese syllabary (*kana* or simplified Japanese char-

[6] Saint Kukai (774-835) was a Japanese Buddhist priest of marvelous versatile gifts. He is also called "Saint Kobo."

[7] Onono Dofu (896-966) is reckoned among the three most distinguished Japanese calligraphers along with Saint Kukai.

acters), Onono Dofu's calligraphy may be nothing. To those who are not pious, prostitutes' popular songs may be more fascinating than Saint Kukai's prayers. To understand a genius, you must understand his make-up.

Yoshisuke: You are right. But I don't see much of merit in Heichu.

Norizane: You see, it's only woman who can tell what the merit of Heichu is. You've just said that ever so many women have been brought to grief by Heichu. But, I'd say that thanks to him ever so many women have appreciated the highest pleasure, have keenly felt their lives worth living and have learned the virtue of sacrifice, and . . .

Yoshisuke: That's enough. Your reasoning would turn a scarecrow into an armed knight.

Norizane: In the green eyes of your jealousy, an armed knight would seem no better than a scarecrow.

Yoshisuke: That's a revelation to me.

Norizane: You don't accuse wanton women as you do Heichu, do you? You may accuse them outwardly, but you don't in your heart. You see, we are men, so jealousy gets into our minds before we are aware of it. We all have a hidden ambition or desire to be more or less of a Heichu. So he is hated more than a traitor. That's unfortunate for him.

Yoshisuke: Then would you like to be a Heichu?

Norizane: Me? No, I don't care for it. So I look at him more fairly than you do. The minute he gets a girl, he gets tired of her, and ridiculously enough, he loses his heart to another girl. That's because he always carries in his heart a vivid image of a Venus or celestial beauty beyond human attainment. He always tries to look for such beauty in earthly women. When he is really in love, he thinks he sees it. But after seeing his ideal image several times in his imagination he loses it. So he wears himself out by his love for one woman after another. In these days there can be no such ideal beauty, so his life cannot but end in misery. In this respect you and I are much happier than he is. Heichu is unhappy because he is a genius. But that is not his only lot. Saint Kukai and Onono Dofu must have had much in common with him. Anyway if you want to be happy, you can do nothing better than be an ordinary man.

GENKAKU-SANBO

CHARACTERS

Genkaku Horikoshi	The consumptive
Otori	Genkaku's wife
Osuzu	Genkaku's daughter
Jukichi	Osuzu's husband
Takeo	Genkaku's grandson
Mme. Kono	The nurse
Oyoshi	Genkaku's mistress
Buntaro	The offspring of Genkaku and Oyoshi
Omatsu	The maid
Oyoshi's brother	A fishmonger
Jukichi's cousin	A university student

The residence "Genkaku [1]-Sanbo" named after the master, "Genkaku Horikoshi," was a snugly built house with graceful gate. In this neighborhood there were not a few such houses to be found. Beyond the wall and the gateplate, which bore the inscription "Genkaku-Sanbo [2]," you could have

[1] "Genkaku" is a highly literary word meaning heavenly crane, but is synonymous with seriousness.
[2] "Sanbo" is also a literary word meaning a hilly residence.

seen plants in the garden which were more artistically laid out than those in any other garden.

The master of this house once was an artist of some renown. He made a fortune by obtaining a patent for his rubber seal and by land-speculation. Some of the real estate which he owned in this fashionable suburb was so barren as not to produce even ginger. Now, the whole neighborhood had grown into a so-called fashionable village lined with semi-foreign style houses roofed with red or blue tiles.

The Genkaku-Sanbo looked all the more picturesque with shapely pine-trees spreading their branches over the fence and with red berries growing on spear flowers planted in front of the gate. The house stood alongside an alley which was so completely deserted that even peddlers merely passed by after discharging their loads and blowing their trumpets into this alley from the thoroughfare.

A long-haired art student, who happened to pass by this house, carrying under his arm an oblong water-color box, asked another student in the same drab uniform, "The Genkaku-Sanbo! What can 'Genkaku' mean?"

"Well, I wonder. It can't possibly be a joke on the word 'seriousness.'"

They both passed the house with light-hearted laughter and left in their wake a faint streak of blue smoke rising from the cigarette butts which they had dropped onto the frozen road.

Jukichi was a bank clerk before he married Genkaku's daughter. By the time he came home from the office, the house was always brightly lit with electric lamps.

For the last few days the moment he entered the gate, he detected a peculiar odor emanating from the breath of Genkaku who was confined to bed with tuberculosis, although it was evident that this offensive odor could not penetrate beyond the house. While walking up the pathway in front of the gate, Jukichi could not but wonder at the sensitivity of his senses.

Genkaku kept to his bed in a separate room, and when he was not lying in bed, he reclined against a stack of padded quilts. Jukichi, after taking off his overcoat and hat, would look in his room and say to him, "How are you today?" or "I'm back now." But he seldom set foot across the threshold into the room, because, he was afraid of catching the disease, and was repelled by the disagreeable odor of Genkaku's breath. Genkaku would say, "Hello!" or "Ah!" in reply. But his words were so feeble that they would be no more than a murmur. Hearing such faint whispers, Jukichi would sometimes feel a pang of conscience for treating his sick father-in-law with such indifference.

Next he would see his mother-in-law, Otori,

who was also confined to bed in the adjoining room. For seven or eight years she had not had the use of her lower limbs, and was unable even to walk to the toilet. He was told that Genkaku had married her primarily because he was greatly attracted by her good looks, and because she was the daughter of the chief retainer of a great feudal lord. In spite of her age, she still retained some lingering beauty in and about her eyes. She looked somewhat like a mummy when she was propped up in bed, darning her white socks with meticulous care. Here again with only such a brief greeting as "How are you today, mother?" he entered the living room.

Jukichi's wife, Osuzu, generally worked in the small kitchen when she was not in the living room. To say nothing of the neat and trim living room, even the kitchen furnished with a gas range was more familiar to Jukichi than the rooms occupied by his bedridden father-in-law and his aging mother-in-law. Jukichi was born the second son of a statesman who was formerly governor of a prefecture. He was a man of talent more like his mother, who was once an accomplished poetess, than his father.

This was expressed in his amiable eyes and slender jaw. Going into the living room, he changed from his foreign suit into a Japanese kimono, sat down at ease in front of the larger brazier, and

smoked a cheap cigar or played with his little boy,
Takeo, his only son, who had entered grade school
that year.

He always sat at the dinner table with his wife,
Osuzu, and Takeo. Their meal was gay and merry.
But recently their happiness had been tinged with
some constraint, because they had in their home a
lodger, a nurse called Kono who was in attendance
on Genkaku. Takeo was as playful as ever and
more so when the nurse was about. From time to
time this made Osuzu knit her brows and frown.
He would goggle his eyes, and in a grandiose manner, continue shoveling the rice from his bowl into
his mouth. Jukichi, who was a great reader of
novels, perceived in the boyish merrymaking, one
who was not entirely innocent of something that
caused displeasure toward him. However, Jukichi
would usually smile and eat his meal in silence.

The nights at the Genkaku-Sanbo were quiet.
Takeo who left home for school early in the morning would go to bed early in the evening. Jukichi
and his wife made a point of going to bed by ten.
The only person who sat up later was the nurse,
Kono, who kept night-watch over the patient. She
would sit up all night by the bedside of Genkaku,
holding her hands over the brazier with its red-hot
charcoal fire. The patient would wake up from
time to time, but he seldom spoke except to tell
her that the hot water-bottle had become cold or

that the cold compress was lukewarm and of little value. In this room nothing was to be heard except the gentle rustle of the bamboo plants. The nurse, watching over him in the chilly quiet, gave thought to various problems: her future and the general feelings of the several members of this family.

One afternoon when the snow had ceased falling, a young woman of twenty-four or twenty-five, together with her slender son, appeared in the Horikoshi family's kitchen furnished with its skylights through which the blue sky could be seen. At that time Jukichi was not, of course, at home. Osuzu, who happened to be working on her sewing machine, had expected such a visit but felt a distinct and embarrassing shock. However, she left the brazier to receive her guest. After coming into the kitchen, the visitor arranged her own clogs and her son's shoes. The boy wore a white sweater. It was evident by these acts that the woman felt insecure and ill at ease. She was Oyoshi, a former maid in this family, whom Genkaku for the last five or six years had openly kept as his mistress in the vicinity of Tokyo.

On seeing her, Osuzu observed that she had prematurely grown old. Her facial appearance was not the only evidence. Four or five years ago her hands were plump and ruddy, but through the passing years they had become emaciated and the veins protruded conspicuously. The sight of her personal apparel, particularly the cheap ring on her finger, impressed Osuzu with the drab insipidness of her wretched domestic life.

"My brother told me to present this to the master," Oyoshi said, and before setting foot in the living room, she furtively put, in a corner of the kitchen, something wrapped in an old newspaper.

The maid, Omatsu, happened to be washing. While her hands were busily employed, she looked askance at Oyoshi, who had her hair dressed in the glossy ginko-leaf style. When she noticed the invisible object wrapped in an old newspaper, a look of suspicion crept into her eyes. It undoubtedly gave forth a horrid odor not in keeping with the smart up-to-date kitchen range or delicate plates and clean dishes.

"Well, this is garlic ma'am," Oyoshi explained, sensing the strange look in Osuzu's face, although she did not look at Omatsu.

"Please, Master Buntaro, bow to the lady," Oyoshi said to her boy who had been biting his finger nails. The boy was of course the offspring of Genkaku and Oyoshi.

Osuzu felt exceedingly sorry for Oyoshi who was in the position to address Buntaro as "Master." But on reflection she realized that this could not be helped. Meantime, looking unperturbed, she served such refreshments as she had in the house to Oyoshi, as well as to her little son who

[151]

had been sitting in a corner of the room. She went on to tell how Genkaku was, and attempted to amuse the child as best she could.

After Genkaku had begun to keep Oyoshi as his mistress, he used to go to see her once or twice a week without minding the extra trouble of having to change trains. At first Osuzu felt an aversion to her father's aberrant sentiments and illicit conduct, and had often wished that he had had a kinder regard for her mother's feelings. But her mother seemed to be completely resigned to the circumstances. This made Osuzu all the more sympathetic towards her. When Genkaku had occasion to visit his mistress, in order to ease her mother's mind, Osuzu would tell her a barefaced lie, such as, "He says he has to attend a poetry meeting today," although she was well aware that her falsehood would do little good. When she read an expression akin to scorn on her mother's face, she would not so much regret that she had perverted the truth as she felt sorry for her paralyzed mother who could not discern her daughter's feelings.

After she had seen her father out, Osuzu would often let her hands fall idle by the sewing machine to ponder over her family. Genkaku was not a kind, respectable father to her, even before he took Oyoshi for his mistress. But that did not matter much to the gentle-natured Osuzu. What worried her was that he took valuable paintings, writings, and curios one after another to his mistress. She had never thought of Oyoshi as a wicked woman after she was employed as a maidservant. On the contrary, she judged that Oyoshi was by nature a little more shy and retiring than ordinary people. However, she could not tell what Oyoshi's brother, who was a fishmonger by trade on the outskirts of Tokyo, was up to. In her eyes he looked like a queer old fox. From time to time Osuzu took the opportunity to confide her apprehension to her husband, Jukichi. But he would be no party to her concern. His answer, "I'm in no position to broach the matter to father," would silence her.

"I'd say that father doesn't think Oyoshi can ever appreciate the pictures by Li Ryan-feng," [3] Jukichi said to Otori once in a while by way of insinuation.

"That's his nature," Otori would say with an ironic smile as she looked up at Jukichi. "Anyway he says even to me, 'What do you think of this *objet d'art?*' I have no knowledge of artistic value, you know."

Later, however, the apprehension proved an absurdity. When Genkaku took a sudden turn for the worse and became too ill to go and see his mistress, a proposal of separation was more readily accepted by Oyoshi than had been anticipated—rather the terms were in reality formulated by

[3] A distinguished Chinese painter of the eighteenth century.

Otori and Osuzu than by Jukichi. Nor was any objection lodged by Oyoshi's brother as had been greatly feared. The terms which were agreed upon provided for an initial payment of two hundred and fifty dollars and an additional monthly remittance of some money for Buntaro's upbringing. Furthermore, before he was asked to, he voluntarily brought back from Oyoshi's house the tea utensils which Genkaku had treasured. Osuzu, who had had misgivings about his character, thought all the better of him.

"My sister says if you're short of hands, she'll be very pleased to come and tend him," Oyoshi's brother said when he brought back the tea things.

Osuzu took counsel with her mother who lay crippled in bed before she accepted this offer of help. It was a step that was later regretted as inconsiderate. On being asked to give advice, Otori recommended that Oyoshi with her little boy, Buntaro, come to help immediately. Osuzu feared that this would result not only in injuring her mother's feelings but in disturbing the atmosphere of the whole family, and she repeatedly asked her mother to reconsider her decision. For all that, as she stood between her father and Oyoshi's brother, she was in the awkward position of being unable to offer a pointblank refusal to his offer of help.

Otori said, "The matter would be different if it hadn't come to my ears. It would be shameful not to have some regard for Oyoshi." Otori would not meekly give way to her daughter. Osuzu was forced to convey to Oyoshi's brother her mother's consent to Oyoshi's coming. This may be said to have been a fault of Osuzu who, after all, knew little of life. When she told this to her husband, Jukichi, who had returned from the office, a frown of displeasure showed between his gentle and somewhat feminine eyebrows.

"Of course, the offer of help must be something for us to be thankful for," Jukichi said. "But I wish you'd have asked father about the matter. Then you wouldn't have been responsible." Osuzu, unusually depressed, replied, "You're right." But it was the last thing she could think of to discuss with her father who was on the verge of death.

While observing Oyoshi and her child, Osuzu remembered such particulars. Oyoshi, without even holding her hands over the glowing fire in the large brazier, talked about her brother and Buntaro, with frequent pauses. She had not yet overcome her provincial accent which had characterized her speech several years ago. Hearing once more her familiar brogue, Osuzu felt somewhat at home in her company, while she vaguely felt somewhat ill at ease about her mother who kept deadly still in the next room, partitioned off by the sliding paper screens.

"Can you stay with us about a week?" Osuzu asked Oyoshi.

[155]

"Yes'm, if you don't mind," was the reply.

"But you will need another kimono, I guess," pursued Osuzu.

"As for a kimono, my brother says he'll bring some over early this evening." While answering her, Oyoshi took a caramel out of her kimono and gave it to the seemingly bored Buntaro.

"I'll go and tell father," said Osuzu. "Now he's so feeble and dejected. He has frostbite on his ear that faces the paper screens near the window." Before leaving the large brazier, Osuzu, without knowing why, reset the iron kettle over the glowing fire.

"Mother," she called. In reply her mother said something in a very feeble voice, as though she had just been awakened by her call.

"Mother, Oyoshi-san [4] is here," Osuzu announced again. Feeling relieved, she stood up promptly in front of the brazier pretending not to see Oyoshi's face. Then passing her mother's room, she said, "Oyoshi-san . . . ," once again.

"Oh, so soon! Good!" replied her mother, who lay in bed covering herself to her lips with the neckband of her quilt, something close to a smile playing in her eyes as she looked up at Osuzu. Osuzu, keenly sensing at her back, that Oyoshi was

[4] "San," the Japanese title of courtesy, corresponding to either, Mr., Mrs., or Miss is affixed after the first as well as to the second name.

following on her heels, hurried nervously to the detached room through the passage opening on to the snow-covered garden.

To the eyes of Osuzu who came in from the bright passage, the detached room seemed to be darker than it really was. Just at that time Genkaku, raised up in bed, was having the nurse read the newspaper.

At the sight of his daughter's face, he suddenly asked, "Oyoshi?" in a husky almost demanding voice.

"Yes," she replied reflectively, as she stood quietly by the sill. After that no one spoke for a few moments.

"I'll tell her to come here right away," Osuzu broke the ice.

"Yes, . . . Is she alone?" asked Genkaku.

"No. . . ."

Genkaku nodded silently.

"Well, Mrs. Kono, come this way, please!" With these words, Osuzu tripped hurriedly through the passage, a step ahead of the nurse. On one of the snow-laden leaves of the palm tree, a wagtail was flicking his tail. She could not help feeling that something uncanny was pressing upon her out of the patient's gloomy room.

Since the arrival of Oyoshi, the atmosphere of the family had grown appreciably more gloomy and melancholy than ever. It started with Takeo teasing Buntaro, who bore a closer resemblance to his mother than to his father and even bore his mother's feminine characteristics. Of course, it was not that Osuzu was unsympathetic with the child, but occasionally considered him as cowardly.

Kono, the nurse, as was required by the nature of her occupation, coldly watched the family tragedy. She seemed rather to enjoy her role as spectator. She was a woman with a dark past. With her sick husband and her intimacies with hospital doctors, she had many times thought of taking a dose of potassium cyanide. Her past implanted in her mind a morbid interest in the sufferings of others. When she came into the family of Genkaku Horikoshi, she found that the crippled Otori did not cleanse her hands even when she responded to the call of nature.

"The young wife of this family is extremely clever. Without arousing suspicion, she takes water for the old woman to cleanse herself." This idea preyed on the mind of the nurse for a while. But in the course of four or five days she discovered that the failure to take water for the old woman to cleanse her hands was an oversight on the part of Osuzu, who had not seen much of life. This discovery gave her something close to satisfaction, and thereafter the nurse took the trouble to take water to the old woman every time she relieved herself.

"Mrs. Kono, how kind of you! I can wash my hands like other people do," Otori exclaimed and clasped her hands together, expressing her thanks in tears. The nurse was not moved at all by Otori's manifestation of joyful gratitude. It was a pleasure for her to see Osuzu placed in a position to carry water to her mother occasionally. Neither was it altogether a displeasure to her, to watch the children quarreling. She behaved before Genkaku as if she were sympathetic with Oyoshi and her child, while before Otori, she feigned resentment toward them. This produced a slow but sure effect.

A week after Oyoshi came to live with the family, Takeo had occasion to fight with Buntaro. The fight started with a dispute as to whether a hog's tail was thicker or thinner than a cow's. Takeo forcibly thrust Buntaro into the corner of his study —a small nine-foot square room—and beat him unmercifully. Oyoshi, who happened to come by just then, took Buntaro, who was hardly able to cry out, into her arms, and began to reprove Takeo.

"Takeo, you mustn't tease the weak," she said in a tone unusually harsh for her quiet nature. Frightened at her threatening attitude, Takeo, crying in turn, ran into the living room. Thereupon, Osuzu, flaring up, abruptly halted her work on the sewing machine, and dragged him forcibly before Oyoshi and her child.

"Takeo, really you're naughty," Osuzu rebuked

her little son. "Now beg the pardon of Oyoshi-san. Humbly beg her pardon on your knees."

Oyoshi sensed that Osuzu really laid the blame at her door, and that all that she could do before the raging Osuzu was to prostrate herself and beg a thousand abject pardons together with her little Buntaro. Inevitably in such cases it was the nurse who acted the part of mediator. While doing her best to persuade the blushing Osuzu to withdraw, the shrewd nurse sneered inwardly imagining what the feelings of Genkaku were, as he silently listened to the brawl. But she did not in any manner betray the slightest sign of her derision.

It was not only the children's squabbles that upset the family peace and quiet. Oyoshi was outwardly stirring the consuming jealousy of Otori who apparently seemed to have been completely resigned to the situation, even though she had not even once been carried away by the green-eyed monster. This was the case with her when Oyoshi used to live in the maid-servant's room five or six years before. But she was prone to vent her pique, in one way or another, on her son-in-law who after all had nothing to do with the affair. This made Osuzu feel extremely sorry for him, and she sometimes apologized to him on behalf of her mother. On such occasions, he would say with a forced smile, "You mustn't get hysterical, either," and changed the subject of the conversation.

The nurse was well aware not only of old Otori's jealousy but of the underlying motive for the old woman's pent-up irritation over Jukichi. In reality, the nurse herself was also consumed by something close to jealousy toward the Jukichi couple before she was aware of it. In her eyes, Osuzu was an unsophisticated daughter; as for Jukichi, he was without doubt a man of well-rounded character, as the common run of people go. But all the same, he was one male that she held in contempt. To her mind, the happiness which such people enjoy was scarcely less than an injustice. With the idea of redressing this injustice, she behaved familiarly with Jukichi. It might have meant nothing to him. Nevertheless, it furnished capital opportunities to ruffle Otori.

"Jukichi," Otori went so far as to make virulent remarks and shamelessly showing her knees, "Aren't you satisfied with my girl—a cripple's daughter?"

But for all that, Osuzu did not seem to be suspicious of Jukichi. On the contrary, she seemed to feel sorry even for the nurse. This not only caused the nurse to be dissatisfied but provoked her to harbor all the more contempt for the good-natured Osuzu. It also gave the nurse the pleasure of seeing that Jukichi had come to avoid her. And it was no less a pleasure to see that, while avoiding her, he had come to feel a manly curiosity about her. Formerly, even in her presence, he did not mind strip-

ping himself bare when taking a bath in the bath-
room beside the kitchen. But recently he had not
let her see him when he was undressed. That was
because he was ashamed of his body, which looked
like a plucked cock. Looking into his face freckled
all over, she wondered, with secret scorn, whom
he expected would fall in love with him other than
his own wife.

One cloudy frosty morning, standing in front of
the mirror set in the small anteroom allotted for
her use, the nurse was combing her hair straight
back as she always did. It was just the day before
Oyoshi was finally going back home. Oyoshi's de-
parture from the family seemed to be an occasion
of joy to the Jukichi couple. It seemed to add all
the more to Otori's irritation. While arranging her
hair, the nurse heard Otori's shrill outcries, and
remembered what a friend had told her about a
certain woman. While the woman lived in Paris,
she experienced intense nostalgia, and availing
herself of a good opportunity offered when her
husband's friend returned home, she boarded a
steamer for home. The long voyage did not seem
to be as trying as she had anticipated. But when
the vessel came within sight of her cherished home-
land off the Kishu Peninsula, she somehow became
suddenly agitated and cast herself into the sea.
The closer she had approached home, the more
acute her nostalgia had become.

Quietly wiping her oily hands, the nurse thought that the self-same mysterious power was at work not only in the jealous feeling of the crippled Otori but also in her own.

"Oh, dear! Mother! What's the matter, crawling so far out here? Mrs. Kono, come and help me, please!" Osuzu's alarm seemed to come from the passage near the detached room. On hearing her outcry, the nurse put on a sneer of contempt, and then as if in surprise, she answered, "Yes, ma'am. Right away."

*　　*　　*　　*　　*　　*　　*

Genkaku grew weaker and weaker. His agonizing suffering from his prolonged illness was intensified by uncomfortable bedsores extending from his back to his loins. With occasional groans, he made futile attempts to mask his suffering. However, it was not only the physical pain that tortured him. During Oyoshi's stay, he could derive some comfort, while on the other hand he had to undergo constant afflictions from his wife's jealousy and his grandchild's quarrels and fights. After Oyoshi left, he felt a devastating loneliness and could not but meditate about his long past desolate life.

"How shameful my life has been!" he reflected. During fleeting moments around the time when he obtained the patent for his rubber seal, and when he passed his days in card-playing and drinking, he could spend comparatively enjoyable days.

Even during that time his companion's envy and his anxiety lest he forfeit his gains constantly harassed him. After he began to keep Oyoshi as his mistress, in addition to his domestic trouble, he was always heavily burdened by his inevitably increased expenses. With all his attachment to the youthful charm of Oyoshi, what a wretch he had been to wish in his heart so many times during the last year or two, that both Oyoshi and her child were dead!

"But I'm not the only one alive to practice this sort of thing," he often thought at night, recalling to his mind the characteristics of his relatives and acquaintances. His son-in-law's father socially murdered a great many of his enemies of inferior ability for allegedly defending constitutional government. An elderly curio dealer, with whom he was on the friendliest terms, formed an illicit intimacy with the daughter of his former wife. A certain lawyer was guilty of embezzlement. And a certain engraver was. . . . Strangely enough, the sins and grave crimes which they committed did not alleviate his own sufferings. On the contrary, they only served to cast dark shadows over his own life.

"Why, my sufferings won't be for long. If I can only go to a better land. . . ." This was the only consolation left to Genkaku. He tried to recall more beautiful memories to erase the torments of those which gnawed deep into his mind and body. He had lived a dark, abject life. If there were a bright side, it would be the memory of his early childhood when he was inexperienced in the cares of life. Between being awake and asleep, he often remembered a certain village hemmed in by the mountains where his parents had lived—above all he recollected the single roof overlaid with stones and the fragrant heap of mulberry leaves to be given to silkworms. But these memories would fade away soon. From time to time between his groanings, he chanted the holy sutras of the Goddess of Mercy, and sang old popular songs of his past days. But it seemed as sacrilegious as it was comical to sing a popular folksong like, "Let's love! Let's love! Over cups of sweet tea!" after chanting the sutra of the Goddess of Mercy, "Omniscient and omnipotent Goddess of Mercy! Cleanse our hearts from sins and deliver us from worldly ills."

"Sleep is a paradise. Sleep is a paradise." He wanted only to sleep and to forget everything.

The nurse, in addition to giving him sleeping pills, continued to give him morphine shots. But his sleep was not always peaceful. Sometimes in his slumber, he met Oyoshi and Buntaro. That made him feel bright and exhilarated. On a certain night as he slept fitfully, he found himself talking to "Cherry-blossom 20" a picture card in his fresh pack of Japanese playing-cards. It had the face of

Oyoshi four or five years ago. Consequently when he awoke, he felt all the more sad and disconsolate. In the course of time, even in his sleep, he came to feel uneasiness and nightmarish horror.

One afternoon as the year was drawing to a close, Genkaku said to the nurse by his bedside, "Mrs. Kono, I haven't worn a loincloth for a long time, so please tell my family to buy me some bleached cotton cloth." However, it was unnecessary for them to take the trouble of despatching the maid to the nearby dry-goods store to get bleached cotton cloth. There was some in the house.

"Thank you. I'll put it on by myself," he said, when he saw the nurse bring some white cotton cloth. "Please fold and leave it here."

He managed to spend the remaining short day, seeking relief from his sufferings by means of this loincloth—clinging to his only hope of hanging himself with it. But being unable even to sit up in bed without another's help, he could not easily seize the opportunity.

Furthermore, he found that at the last moment death was dreadful to him. In the dim electric light, looking at a line of Chinese calligraphy written on the hanging scroll, he berated himself for still frantically clinging to life.

"Mrs. Kono, just raise me, please," he said around ten at night. "I'll sleep, so please go to bed without attending me, won't you?"

"No, thank you. I'll keep awake," the nurse replied calmly, gazing at him in wonder. "This is my duty, sir."

He felt that she had seen through his plan. But with a slight nod, he shammed sleep by refraining from saying anything. The nurse, spreading out the January issue of a woman's magazine, kept on reading it intently by his bedside.

Genkaku, thinking of the loincloth, watched the nurse through slitted eyes. Then he suddenly felt amused.

"Mrs. Kono," he called the nurse. She looked really stunned when she beheld his face. Leaning upon the quilts, he was convulsed with laughter.

"May I help you?"

"No, thank you. There's nothing amusing." Still tittering, he replied, shaking his lean right arm.

"Now . . . somehow I feel amused. . . . Now lay me on my side, please."

About an hour later he fell fast asleep. That night he had a shuddering nightmare. Standing amidst luxuriant foliage, he was peeping into a room, which looked like a tea-ceremony arbor, through an opening between the sliding paper-screens. There he discovered a child stark naked lying down, with his face directed towards him. Although a child, he was as wrinkled and withered as an old man. Trying to cry out, he awoke, bathed in perspiration.

[167]

He found no one in his room and it was still dark. Evidently it was not yet the time. Looking at the table-clock, he found that it was getting on towards twelve. Momentary relief flooded his mind. But he soon reverted to his usual gloom. Lying on his back, he counted his respirations. He felt as though he were oppressed by a solemn voice repeating, "Now is the time." Softly drawing the loincloth towards him, he coiled it around his neck, and pulled both ends with his hands.

Just then Takeo, bundled up like a dumpling, showed up.

"Wow! Grandpa's doing something," and frightened, he ran in desperation toward the living room.

*   *   *   *   *   *   *

A week later surrounded by his family, Genkaku breathed his last, a victim of tuberculosis. His funeral was a grand and imposing ceremony attended by a large number of mourners, among whom the absence of his wife who had lost the use of her limbs was conspicuous. After expressing their sympathy to the Jukichi couple, they burned incense in front of his coffin which was adorned with white satin. With the exception of his staunch old friends, by the time they left the gate, they had mostly forgotten about him.

"He must have lived a happy life," all the

mourners declared. "Anyway he had a young mistress and made a sizable fortune, you know."

A horse-drawn funeral carriage, in the lingering light of the late December sun, rolled toward a crematory along a street. Those riding in the drab carriage following were Jukichi and his cousin.

His cousin, a university student, was concerned about the jolting of the carriage, as he was intent on reading a small-sized book, without talking much to Jukichi. It was the English translation of Wilhelm Liebknecht's "Reminiscences." On the way Jukichi often dozed off because of the previous night's vigil. While looking out onto the newly-built street, he said to himself half-heartedly, "This part of town has changed drastically."

The two carriages, rumbling along the slushy road at last reached the crematory. On inquiry, they found that although they had made previous arrangements over the telephone, the first-class furnaces were already occupied and there were only some second-class ones vacant. That did not matter much to them. But out of deference to the wishes of Osuzu rather than to those of the departed, Jukichi negotiated earnestly with the clerk who was on the other side of the half-moon shaped window.

"To tell you the truth, his case was too far gone when he was placed under medical care, so I do hope that he'll be cremated first-class at least." He

[169]

went so far as to make this false representation just for a try. This seemed to produce a greater effect than he had expected.

"Let's settle it this way," the clerk replied. "Since the first-class ones are full, we'll cremate him special class at the same expense as for a first-class one."

A little embarrassed, Jukichi thanked the clerk repeatedly.

"You're quite welcome," said the clerk, who, with his brass spectacles, looked like a good-natured old man.

After sealing the furnace, they were about to leave the gate of the crematorium when Oyoshi who had been standing alone outside the brick wall nodded toward their carriage. A little upset, Jukichi tried to raise his hat in answer. By that time the carriage was already rumbling along a steep road bordered by bare poplar trees.

"That's she, isn't it?"

"Yes, I was looking only at the beggars... What's she going to do from now on, I wonder."

"Well, I, too, wonder..." Jukichi replied as indifferently as possible, as he lit a cigarette.

His cousin turned silent. But Jukichi's imagination conjured up the picture of a certain fishing village in Chiba Prefecture, where Oyoshi and her child would have to live. His cousin suddenly assumed a sullen look and began reading Liebknecht once again.

OTOMI'S VIRGINITY

AT A LITTLE PAST NOON, May 14, 1868, in the city
of Edo, a notice was posted, reading: "At dawn tomorrow the Imperial Army will attack the 'Shogi-
tai' entrenched in Toei Hill. Civilians living in
the vicinity of Ueno should take refuge anywhere
they can."

Inside the house evacuated by Masabei Kogaya,
a grocer, at Mi-chome, Shitaya-machi, a tortoise-
shell colored cat was crouching in front of a large
sea-shell in the corner of the kitchen. The house
was so tightly shuttered that even in broad daylight
it was dark and quiet inside. The only sound was
the pattering of the rain that had been falling for
days. From time to time a heavy downfall poured
upon the roof and each time the sound grew louder,
the cat raised her amber eyes—eyes that gave off
an ominous phosphorescent glow in the room so
dark that even the stove was not discernible. Finding that no change occurred except in the pattering
of the rain, the cat stayed still, but narrowed her
eyes thread-thin.

Repeating this action again and again, she must have fallen asleep, for soon she stopped opening her eyes at all. The rain continued to fall heavily and to ease, alternately. Three o'clock . . . Four o'clock . . . The time gradually passed into dusk amidst the sound of the rain.

When five o'clock came, the cat suddenly rounded her eyes and pin-pointed them, as if something had frightened her. The rain had subsided, and nothing was audible but the cries of sedan-carriers running down the street. After several seconds of silence, the kitchen suddenly became dimly lighted. Then into view, object by object, came the kitchen-stove, the sparkling of the water in a lidless jar, the kitchen shrine, and the rope for opening the skylight. Looking all the more uneasy, the cat slowly raised her large body and glared at the outer door, which had just been opened.

The person who opened the door at that moment—not only the outer door, but also the inner, paper door—was a beggar as wet as a drowned rat. Stretching his neck, which was wrapped in an old towel, he listened stealthily and attentively for any possible noise in the quiet house. After making sure that there was not a soul within, he went into the kitchen, his new straw raincoat bright with rain. Flattening her ears, the cat recoiled a few steps. Paying no attention to the cat for the moment, the beggar slid the paper door closed behind him and slowly unwrapped the towel from around his neck. His uncut hair was extremely long, and he had a couple of adhesive paper bandages on his face. Although he was very dirty, he had rather regular features.

"Pussy, pussy," he said in a low tone, wiping his hair and face, which were dripping with rain. The cat pricked up her ears as though she recognized his voice. But staying where she was, she fixed suspicious eyes upon him at intervals. Meanwhile, the beggar took off his raincoat, sat down on the floor in front of the cat, and crossed his legs, which were so muddy that the color of his shins was hardly visible.

"How do you do, pussy?" he asked, laughing to himself and stroking the cat on the head. "Seeing nobody's here, I'd say they've left you in the lurch." For a second the cat seemed about to poise on tiptoe for flight, but she did not spring away. On the contrary, she remained sitting, but gradually began to narrow her eyes. When he had stopped stroking the cat, the beggar took an oiled pistol out of his pocket and started examining its trigger in the twilight. The beggar, handling his pistol in the kitchen of the deserted house in an atmosphere of threatening war—this certainly was an unusual and curious sight! Yet, with her eyes narrowed and her back humped, the cat remained sitting as indifferently as though she knew all secrets.

[173]

"Hey, pussy," the beggar said to the cat; "to-morrow showers of bullets will fall in this neighborhood. If you're hit, you'll die. So no matter how great a tumult breaks out, don't stir out of the house, and lie hidden under the floor.

"We've been pals. But this will be the last I'll see of you," he said to the cat from time to time, while examining his pistol. "Tomorrow may be an evil day for both you and me. Tomorrow I may die, too. Even if I get off unhurt, I won't hunt around rubbish heaps any more, and you'll be mighty happy, won't you?"

In the meantime the sound of the rain was louder. The clouds were close enough to obscure the roof tiles. The twilight which had hung over the kitchen grew darker and fainter than ever. The beggar, without raising his face, started to load his pistol which he had finished examining.

"Will you miss me any when I'm gone?" he went on. "No, cats forget three years' kindness, they say, so I guess you can't be trusted, either.— Well, that doesn't matter. But when I'm gone, too. . . ."

The beggar suddenly was silent, for he heard someone stepping up to the outside of the outer door. He thought someone stepped up to the outer door simultaneously with his putting away his pistol, and just as he looked back, the backdoor was thrust open. Quicker than thought, he assumed the posture of defense, and soon the beggar and the intruder were looking straight at each other.

The instant the incomer saw the beggar, she gave an outcry of sudden surprise. She was a barefooted young woman, holding a paper umbrella in her hand. She had an almost impulsive desire to dash back into the rain, but at last regaining her courage after her first astonishment, she tried to look into the beggar's face through the little bit of light in the kitchen.

In blank amazement, the beggar watched her closely, raising one knee under his *yukata* (unlined kimono.) His look showed that he was no longer on his guard. For a while the two silently looked at each other face to face.

"You're Shinko, aren't you?" she asked the beggar recovering some of her composure.

"Oh, pardon me," the beggar said with a grin, and bobbed his head a couple of times towards her. "The heavy shower just drove me into your house in your absence. I haven't turned housebreaker, I assure you."

"I'm really surprised. Even if you are not a housebreaker, you carry your impudence too far," she cried out in vexation, swishing water off her umbrella. "Now get out of here. I'm coming in."

"Yes, I'll go without your ordering me to. Haven't you taken refuge yet, miss?"

"Yes, I have. Why not? But what does it matter?"

"Then you left something, I guess. Now come right in here. You're exposed to the rain out there."

As if still exasperated, without giving any reply to his remark, she sat down on the kitchen floor. Stretching her dirty feet, she began ladling water on her dirty feet. Then the beggar, who sat crossed-legged with full composure, stared fixedly at her, stroking his shaggy-bearded chin. She was a buxom country brunette with pimples on her nose. She wore a plain homespun garment and a cotton sash, as befitting a young maid. Her lively features and attractive figure had an irresistible charm.

"Since you have come back in this confusion, you must have left something very important," he went on asking. "What did you leave? Eh? Miss . . . Otomi-san?"

"Mind your own business. First of all, get out at once, I tell you."

Otomi's answer was blunt. Looking up into his face, she started questioning him with a serious look, as if she had thought of something.

"Shinko," she said, "do you know where our pussy is?"

"Pussy? She was here just now," he said, looking around. "Oh, dear! Where could she have gone?"

The cat had crept up to the shelf unnoticed and was crouching between an earthenware mortar and an iron pot. Otomi caught sight of the cat at the same moment as Shinko. Instantly Otomi threw away her dipper, and stood up on the floor as though she had forgotten the beggar's presence. And with a bright smile, she called the cat on the shelf. Shinto shifted his curious eyes from the cat to Otomi.

"Is it the cat that you left, miss?"

"Why shouldn't it be a cat? Pussy, pussy, now come down."

Shinko suddenly burst out laughing. His laughter called forth an eerie echo amidst the resounding noise of the rain. Otomi, quite surprised, shouted at Shinko out of her renewed vexation, with her cheeks all flushed.

"What makes you laugh? The mistress is upset about having left her cat behind. Worried about the life of the cat, she has been crying all the while. Out of pity for her I've come back all the way in the rain . . ."

"All right. I won't laugh any more." Still continuing to laugh, Shinko interrupted Otomi's remark. "I won't laugh any more. But just think of it. When war may break out tomorrow, a mere cat or two—it is funny, whatever one thinks about it. With all deference to your presence, let me take the liberty of telling you the mistress here is the most unreasonable and selfish woman I've ever heard of. First of all, to look for her pussy . . ."

"Shut up!" Otomi exclaimed with a threatening look, "I don't like to hear you slander my mistress."

As might be expected, the beggar was not frightened by her threatening countenance. On the contrary he had been fixing a rude look upon her person. Her figure at that moment was really savage beauty itself. Her rain-wet *yukata* and petticoat were stuck fast to her skin and her bare soft virginal body was transparent. Shinko, with his eyes fixed upon her, continued to talk laughingly.

"Above anything else, you can tell it by her sending you here to look for the pussy. Now every family in the vicinity of Ueno has already taken refuge. The people's houses are as deserted as uninhabited fields. No wolves may possibly come out, but there's no knowing what terrible danger you may meet with."

"Don't worry unnecessarily, and catch the cat quickly. I don't expect war will break out. How could there be any danger?"

"Don't talk nonsense. If there's no danger in a young girl's walking alone, there can be no danger whatever," Shinko gradually began talking in a vein half-serious and half-jocular. "Coming to the point, we're only two of us here. If I should have a funny desire, what would you do, miss?"

There was not a shadow of fear in Otomi's eyes,

[178]

but her cheeks were flushed with more blood than ever.

"What, Shinko?—Do you mean to threaten me?" Otomi shouted, taking a step up to his side, as though she were threatening him.

"Threaten?" he retorted. "Lots of titled people are rotten and ill-mannered. Moreover, I'm a beggar. I may do more than threaten. If I really got a funny desire, . . ."

Before he had finished, he was knocked heavily on the head. Before he was aware of it, Otomi was brandishing her umbrella in front of him.

"Don't talk fresh!" Again she struck him on the head with her umbrella with all her might. He tried to dodge the blows but at that instant her umbrella hit him hard on his shoulder which was covered only with a hemp garment. Aroused, the cat, kicking down an iron kettle, sprang upon the shelf where the family kitchen shrine was placed. At the same time the pine branch and the oil lamp on the shelf fell down on Shinko. Before he could spring to his feet, he was repeatedly slugged with Otomi's umbrella.

"Damn you! Damn you!" she cried and continued to brandish her umbrella. Finally, he succeeded in snatching the umbrella from her.

No sooner had he thrown off the umbrella than he furiously sprang upon her. For a while the two grappled with each other on the small wooden floor. Amidst this scuffle the shower, gathering in strength, battered the roof. As the sound of the rain became louder, the dusk deepened moment by moment. Beaten and scratched, the beggar furiously strove to overpower and hold her down by his physical strength. The instant he seized hold of her after repeated failures, he dashed toward the entrance like a shot.

"You damned bitch!" he glared at her fiercely with the sliding screen as his shield.

With her hair already disheveled, Otomi, sat down flat on the floor, grasping a razor in her hand with the blade down. Presumably she had brought it in her sash. Her grim look and strange maidenly charm was like that of the cat with her back rounded on the shelf of the shrine. Remaining silent for a few seconds, they studied each other's eyes. Then wearing an affected grin, Shinko took the pistol out of his pocket.

"Now struggle as you will," he said, deliberately aiming the muzzle of his pistol at her chest. Although she looked at him regretfully, she did not open her mouth. Noting her silence, he directed the muzzle higher as if he had thought of something. In front of the muzzle, gleamed the amber-colored eyes of the cat.

"All right, Otomi-san?" he asked in a voice pregnant with a smile as if to tease her.

"If I fire this pistol, the cat'll drop headlong

dead." He was on the point of pulling the trigger. "It'll be the same with you. Agreed?"

"Don't!" Otomi suddenly cried out. "Shinko, don't fire!"

Shinko shifted his eyes towards her, with his pistol still aimed at the tortoise-shell cat.

"Of course, I guess you'll be sorry."

"It's a pity to shoot her. For mercy's sake, don't." Now a complete change came over Otomi. Her eyes showed her concren. Through her slightly trembling lips showed a row of fine teeth. With a look of half-derision and half-wonder, the beggar lowered the muzzle. This brought a look of relief over the girl's face.

"Well, I'll spare the cat. In place of it..." he triumphantly declared. "In place of it I'll just take you."

Otomi turned her eyes away. For that instant her inmost heart seemed to seethe in a turmoil of various feelings: hatred, anger, disgust, and grief. Keeping a careful watch over these expressions, he walked sidewise behind her back, and threw open the paper sliding-doors of the living room, which was still darker than the kitchen. In this room, the chest of drawers and the oblong charcoal brazier loomed up distinctly. The empty room clear of anything else imparted a vivid impression of the evacuation. Standing behind Otomi, he dropped his eyes to her neck which looked

[181]

slightly moist with perspiration. She may have sensed it. Twisting her body, she looked up into his face. The lively color, just as before, was already back in her face. However, as if he were very confused, giving a queer blink, he turned his pistol again at the cat.

"Don't! I tell you, don't!" Trying to stop him, she dropped the razor which she had held in her hand.

"If I mustn't, go over there," he said with a faint smile.

"Oh, you're nasty," she grumbled in vexation. But getting up, she hurriedly went into the living room in the manner of an indelicate woman. He looked somewhat astonished at her complete resignation to her fate. The noise of the rain had already greatly subsided by that time. Moreover, the breaks in the clouds might have been lit by the glow of the setting sun. The kitchen, which had been gloomy, gradually grew lighter. Standing in the kitchen, he listened carefully to the sound of rustling in the living room, her untying of her cotton sash, and presumably her lying down on the mat. After that the living-room became deadly still.

After some apparent hesitation, he set foot in the dimly lit living room. In the middle of the room he found her lying still on her back, her face covered with her sleeves. The moment he saw her, he scurried back to the kitchen. His face had a strange, indescribable expression, which looked like disgust or shame. The minute he was back in the kitchen, he started laughing, with his back still turned toward the living room.

"I've been teasing you, Otomi-san," he cried out. "I've been teasing. Now come out here, please."

Some minutes later Otomi, with the cat in her bosom and her umbrella in her hand, was talking cheerfully with Shinko, who was sitting on a small thin mat.

"Miss!" he asked, without daring to look her in the face as if he were still embarrassed, "I have something I'd like to ask you."

"What is it?"

"Well, nothing particularly serious," he quibbled. "But you see, it's a matter of vital importance in a woman's life to give herself to a man. You Otomi-san ... in exchange for the cat's life. Anyway that was too reckless of you, Otomi-san, wasn't it?" He held his tongue for a minute. Otomi, with a smile beaming all over her face, gave no answer, only caressed the cat in her bosom.

"Do you love the cat so much?"

"Yes, I do love the cat," she answered vaguely.

"Well, you've got a fine reputation in the neighborhood for your faithful service to your master. Were you afraid that you'd be terribly sorry for your mistress if the cat were killed?"

"Well, I love pussy, and to be sure my mistress

is important to me, but I . . ." Inclining her head slightly on one side, she behaved as though she were looking far away. "Well, how should I put it? I somehow felt I must act like that. That's all."

Several minutes later, left alone, Shinko was squatting absent-mindedly in the kitchen, with his hands on his knees under his old hempen garment. Amidst a sprinkling of rain, evening dusk had been gradually closing in around where he was. The rope of the skylight, the water-jar by the sink, sank out of sight one by one, when the sporadic temple-bells of Ueno, pent up by the rain clouds, began pealing their heavy gongs. As if surprised at the sound, he looked about his surroundings enveloped in dead silence. Then groping his way to the sink, he filled a dipper with water.

"Shinsaburo Shigemitsu, surnamed Muragami, son of the old House of Minamoto as I am, I've suffered a blow today." So grumbling, he enjoyed his fill of water.

*　　*　　*　　*　　*　　*　　*

The 26th March, 1889, saw Otomi and her husband walking with their three children on the boulevard of Ueno.

That was the very day when the opening ceremony of the third national exposition was held at Takenodai, Ueno. And, the cherry blossoms around the entrance to Ueno Park were mostly all out. So the boulevard of Ueno was hustling and bustling with immense crowds of people. From the direction of Ueno there were constant streams of coaches and *jinrikisha* (man-pulled carts) coming on their way home from the opening ceremony. Among the passengers of these vehicles were prominent people, such as Masana Maeda, Ukichi Taguchi, Eiichi Shibusawa, Shinji Tsuji, Kakuzo Okakura, and Masao Gejo.

His eldest son holding onto his sleeve, Otomi's husband was carrying his five-year-old second son in his arms, and dodging his way through the congestion of the pedestrian and vehicular traffic, from time to time he anxiously looked back at Otomi leading her daughter by the hand. Otomi threw him a radiant smile each time. Of course the lapse of the intervening twenty years had brought her a certain maturity. But her eyes were just as clear and bright as in her former years. Around 1870 she had married her present husband, nephew to Furukawaya, Seibei. He kept a small watch store first in Yokohama and now on Ginza Street, Tokyo.

Otomi happened to look up, and saw Shinko sitting leisurely in a two-horse carriage which happened to be passing by. She was particularly attracted to his breast which appeared to be buried under various badges of honor—many large and small decorations, gold-laced stripes, and peacock feathers. Nevertheless, it was beyond doubt that this ruddy gray-bearded face looking at her was that of the former beggar. She slackened her pace in spite of herself. But strangely enough, she was not surprised. Somehow she had known that he was no mere beggar. She might have observed this by his countenance, language, or the pistol he carried. She fixed her gaze intently on his face. Whether intentionally or accidentally he was also closely watching hers. At that instant her memory of twenty years ago was awakened with painful distinctness. On that far-away day she had imprudently resigned herself to giving herself up to him to save the cat's life. What was her motive then? She could not tell. In such a situation he could not persuade himself even to touch the body which she had surrendered to him. What was his motive then? She could not tell that either. Although she could not tell, that was all too natural to her. Crossing his carriage, she felt her mind relieved of all her cares.

When the carriage had passed by, Otomi's husband looked over at her through the dense throng of people. Looking back at him cheerfully and happily, Otomi smiled as though nothing had happened.

THE SPIDER'S THREAD

1

ONE GLORIOUS DAY in Paradise, Buddha was strolling along the rim of the Lotus Pond. The lotus flowers in all their glory were pearly white with an exquisite fragrance flowing constantly from the golden-tinted pistils and stamens in their centers. It was morning in Paradise.

Presently the merciful Buddha, pausing by the fringe of the pond, happened to peep down through the lotus leaves overgrowing the surface of the pond. Deeply submerged beneath the Lotus Pond lay the shadowy abyss of Hell. Down through the crystal-clear water one could see the scenes of the River Styx and the Mountain of Needles as vividly as though one were peering through an underwater glass boat.

There at the lowest recesses of Hell, he saw a man named Kandata writhing together with his fellow sinners. He was a notorious robber who had set houses on fire, committed murders and many other wicked crimes. But, he retained in his memory the recollection of one good deed in his life. This is how it happened: One day while walking through a dense forest, he caught sight of a spider creeping along by the side of the path. He had an impulse to lift up his foot and crush it. A nobler thought, however, crossed his mind. "Although it is only an insignificant creature, life must be dear to it. Also, it would be too cruel of me to take its little life for no purpose or good reason," he said to himself, and let it hurry away to safety.

While surveying Hell beneath, Buddha remembered how he had once spared the spider's life, and in reward for his good deed, he thought of giving Kandata a chance of escaping from Hell.

Fortunately at that very moment he saw, close at hand a spider of Paradise weaving its beautiful silvery silken web on the jade-green lotus leaves. Taking the spider's thread softly in his hand, he let it fall through an opening amid the pearly white lotus leaves straight down to the very bottom of Hell.

2

In the Pool of Blood down at the very bottom of Hell, Kandata was found to be bobbing up-and-down with the other sinners. Indeed, at the bottom of Hell, wherever one might look, it was as dark as night, and nothing else was to be seen but sporadic gleamings of pointed needles jutting sharply from the ghostly Mountain of Needles. The sight of the foundation of Hell was desolate and gruesome beyond all words. Moreover, all around the eerie place was as still as a graveyard, and nothing could be heard but the faint sighs and heavy groans that come every now and then from the parched lips of deadly sinners in miserable torment, for the human beings who fall to the very bottom of Hell are so tired and worn out by the thousand and one tortures, that they have no strength left even to cry out. Such being the case, incorrigible robber as he was, Kandata was struggling and squirming like a dying frog, choked with blood in the Pool of Blood.

One day, he happened to raise his head and look up into the gloomy sky. Then what should he see but the silvery white thread of a spider slipping gradually down toward him trailing a slender glimmering ray of light as stealthily as though it feared to be caught sight of by the vigilant eyes of the damned.

At the sight of this delicate thread, he clapped his hands for joy. If he could but cling to this thread and climb up higher and higher to its very starting point, he would be sure to get out of Hell. Yes, if things were to go well, by good luck he might possibly be able even to get into Paradise. Then no longer would he be cast upon the prickly

Mountain of Needles or plunged into the deathly Pool of Blood.

With this idea in mind, he grasped the thread tightly in both hands, and instantly pulling himself up hand over hand with all his might, he soon began to rise higher and higher. As he was a notorious burglar in his time, he must have been perfectly adept at this sort of thing.

However, Paradise is millions of miles higher up than Hell, so although he made the most strenuous efforts, he could not go up a long way as he had eagerly sought to do. He had been climbing up for some time when he became so utterly tired that he did not have the strength left to haul himself another inch. Since there was nothing he could do but rest for a while, clinging fast to the dangling thread, he looked down below.

Then how well he thanked his good fortune for his hard and laborious climb! He now saw the Pool of Blood, in which he had been wallowing till but a little while ago, obscurely hidden beneath the dark and terrible Mountain of Needles faintly gleaming below his feet. If he could go on with his successful ascent at his present rapid rate, he might escape from Hell even more easily than he at first expected. Lacing both his hands around the spider's slender thread, he exclaimed, "I've done it!" and laughed louder than he had done in many years. Then suddenly right down below him he noticed

a countless number of his fellow sinners clamber-
ing up the same thread close on his heels like an
endless procession of ants. At this sight, he was
struck with both amazement and paralytic fear, his
eyes goggling and his mouth agape like a fool in a
trance. How could this spider's almost invisible
thread, which at any moment might snap even
under his own weight, ever support the heavy
weight of so many? What if the thread should snap
off halfway? Then he himself who had climbed so
far up after all his desperate efforts would be hurled
back head first into his former despondency in
Hell. Then all would be over with him. Even in
the meantime, thousands upon thousands of sinners were clearly seen struggling up, in a single
line, along the slender silvery thread, after squirming and wriggling out of their dark Pool of Blood
like so many filthy worms. If nothing were done
at once before it was too late, the thread would
soon be cut off halfway, and then, surely enough,
once again he would hurtle headlong to the very
bottom of Hell.

"You damned sinners!" Kandata shouted in his
loudest voice. "This spider's thread is mine. Who
told you to climb up? Get down! All of you get
down!"

Just at that instant the spider's thread, which
had been steady enough, suddenly gave way just
where he had been clutching it, with the result you

might well imagine. In a twinkling Kandata hurtled downwards head over heels into the murky abyss of Hell. And behind him nothing was left but the slender gleams of the spider's thread hanging aloft in the pitch-dark sky bereft of moon and stars.

3

Standing on the edge of the Lotus Pond, Buddha had been observing all that was happening in the world below. When he saw Kandata sink to the bottom of the Pool of Blood like a heavy stone, he looked sorrowful and walked away.

The black heart of Kandata, which sought only for his own way out of Hell at the expense of all the others finally to bring about his own downfall, must have been a miserable shame in the eyes of Gautama Buddha.

Little, however did the lotus flowers in Paradise care about the happenings in the nether world. All this while the pearly white lotus flowers kept waving their green calyces around the feet of their merciful Lord, with the exquisite fragrance from their golden pistils and stamens in their centers constantly perfuming the clear air all around. In Paradise it must be getting on towards noon.

THE NOSE

In the town of Ike-no-O [1] there was no one who had not heard of Zenchi Naigu's [2] nose. Dangling from his upper lip to below his chin, five or six inches long, it was of the same thickness from end to end.

For fifty years he had been tormented at heart by the presence of his nose—from his young days as an acolyte until the time he rose to the respected office of Palace Chaplain. To others he tried to appear unconcerned about his nose, not so much because his preoccupation with such a matter was not worthy of a man whose duty it was to devote himself ardently to prayer for the advent of Paradise as because he wished to keep from the knowledge of others that he was worried over his nose. With him his apparent concern was rather

[1] Ike-no-O—place name of Uji District in Kyoto.
[2] Zenchi Naigu—Son of Tamibe Shosuke. Naigu is short for Naigubuso who were ten chosen priests of high character in service at the Imperial Court, praying for the Emperor's good health.

a matter of pride, and his greatest dread in every-day conversation was to hear the word, nose.

His nose was, of course, an intolerable nuisance. In the first place, he could not take his meals by himself. If he tried, the tip of his nose would reach down into the boiled rice in his bowl. So at meals he had to have one of his disciples sit opposite him and hold up the end of his nose with an oblong piece of wood about two feet long and an inch wide. This manner of taking meals was, of course, no easy matter for the priest whose nose was held up or for his disciple who held it up.

Once a page, who was acting in the place of the disciple, happened to sneeze and dropped the nose into the bowl—this incident was talked about as far as Kyoto. He could accept the practical inconvenience of having a long nose, but the loss of his dignity on account of it was intolerable.

The Ike-no-O townspeople used to say that it was fortunate for the priest that he was not a lay-man, for surely no woman would care to be the wife of a man who had such a nose. Some went so far as to say that were it not for his nose, he might not have taken holy orders.

He did not consider that his priesthood had been a refuge which offered him any service in lightening the burden of his nose. Moreover his pride was too delicately strung for him to be influenced in the least by such a worldly eventuality as matrimony.

His sole concern was to resort to every possible means to heal the wounds his pride had suffered and to repair the losses his dignity had sustained.

He exhausted all possible means to make his nose appear shorter than it really was. When there was no one about, he would examine his nose in the mirror and look at it from various angles, taxing his ingenuity to the utmost. Just changing the reflections of his face in the mirror was not enough: prodding his cheeks, or putting his finger on the tip of his chin, he would patiently study his face in the mirror. But not once could he satisfy himself that his nose was shorter. Indeed, it often happened that the more he studied his nose the longer it seemed to be. On such occasions, he would put his mirror back into its box, sighing heavily, and sadly going back to his lectern would continue chanting the sutra to Kwannon or the Goddess of Mercy.

He paid close attention to other people's noses. The Temple of Ike-no-O, frequented by a large number of visitors, both priests and laymen, held Buddhist masses, receptions for visiting priests and sermons for parishioners. The precincts of the Temple were lined with closely built cells, with a bathhouse which had heated water daily. He would closely scrutinize the visitors, patiently trying to find at least one person who might possibly have a nose like his own in order that he might ease his troubled mind. He took no notice of the rich silken attire, the ordinary hempen clothes, the priests' saffron hoods nor their dark sacerdotal robes, all of which counted for next to nothing in his eyes. That which arrested his eyes was not the people or their attire but their noses. He could find hooked noses but none like his own. Each additional failure made his thinking darker and gloomier.

While talking with others, unconsciously he would take between his fingers the tip of his dangling nose; then he would blush with shame for an act ill-fitting his years and office. His misfortune had driven him to such extremes.

In his desperate attempt to find some consolation by discovering someone with a nose like his own, he delved into the voluminous Buddhist scriptures; but in all the scriptures there was not one reference to a long nose. How comforting it would have been to find, for instance, that either Mu Lien [3] or Sha Lien [4] had a long nose.

He did find that King Liu Hsan-ti [5] of the Kingdom of Chu-han in the third century A.D. had long ears, and thought how reassuring it would

[3] Mu Lien—one of Shakyamuni's principal disciples; he was possessed of occult powers.
[4] Sha Li Hsien—another of Shakyamuni's disciples he was renowned for his broad knowledge.
[5] King Liu Hsan-ti (A.D. 160-223) had long ears according to the "Shih-pa-shih-liieh" (A History of Ancient China).

have been if it had happened that the King's nose, instead of his ears, had been long.

It need hardly be said that while taking assiduous pains to seek spiritual consolation, he did try most earnestly a variety of elaborate practical measures to shorten his nose. At one time he took a concoction with a snake-gourd base. At another he bathed his nose in the urine of mice; yet with all his persistent and unremitting efforts, he still had five to six inches of nose dangling down over his lips.

One autumn day a disciple went on a trip to Kyoto, partly on his master's business, and before his returning to Ike-no-O, his physician acquaintance happened to introduce him to the mysteries of shortening noses. The physician, who had come to Japan from China, was at that time a priest attached to the Choraku Temple.

Zenchi, with an assumed nonchalance, avoided calling for an immediate test of the remedy, and could only drop casual hints about his regret that he must cause his disciple so much bother at meals, although he eagerly waited in his heart for his disciple to persuade him to try the remedy. The disciple could not fail to see through his master's design. But his master's innermost feelings, which led him to work out such an elaborate scheme, aroused his disciple's sympathy. As Zenchi had expected, his disciple advised him to try this method with such extraordinary urgency that, according to his premeditated plan, he finally yielded to his earnest counsel.

The formula was a simple one: first to boil the nose in hot water, and then to let another trample on it and torment it.

At the Temple bath-house water was kept "at the boil" daily, so his disciple brought in an iron ladle, water so hot that no one could have put a finger into it. It was feared that Zenchi's face would be scalded by steam; so they bored a hole in a wooden tray and used the tray as a lid to cover the pot so that his nose could be immersed in the boiling water. As for his nose, no matter how long it was soaked in the scalding water, it was immune from ill-effect.

"Your Reverence," the disciple said after awhile, "I suppose it must be sufficiently boiled by now."

The Chaplain, with a wry smile, was thinking that no one who overheard this remark could suspect that it concerned a remedy for shortening his nose.

Heated by water and steam, his nose itched as if bitten by mosquitoes.

When the nose was withdrawn from the hole in the lid, the disciple set about trampling on that steaming object, exerting all his strength in pounding it with both his feet. Zenchi, lying on his side, and stretching his nose on the floor-boards, watched his disciple's legs move up-and-down.

"Does it hurt, Your Reverence?" his disciple asked from time to time, looking down sympathetically on the priest's bald head. "The physician told me to trample hard on it. Doesn't it hurt?"

Zenchi tried to shake his head by way of indicating that he was not feeling any pain, but as his nose was being trampled on he could not do this, so rolling his eyes upwards, in a tone that suggested he was offended, and with his gaze fixed on his disciple's chapped feet, he said, "No, it doesn't hurt." Although his itching nose was being trampled on, it was a comfortable rather than a painful sensation.

His nose having undergone this treatment for some time, what seemed to be grains of millet began to appear, at which sight his disciple stopped trampling and said in soliloquy, "I was told to pull them out with tweezers."

The nose looked like a plucked and roasted chicken. With cheeks puffed out, though disgruntled, the priest suffered his disciple to deal with his nose as the man saw fit,—although, however aware of his disciple's kindness he might have been, he did not relish his nose being treated as if it were a piece of inert matter. Like a patient undergoing an operation at the hands of a surgeon in whom he does not place implicit trust, Zenchi reluctantly watched his disciple extract from the pores of his nose, feathers of fat, curled to half-an-inch in diameter. The treatment finished, the disciple looked relieved and said: "Now, your Reverence, we have only to boil it once more, and it'll be all right."

Zenchi, with knit brow, submitted to the treatment meted out to him.

When his nose was taken out of the pot for the second time, it was found, to their great surprise, remarkably shorter than before and was not very different from a normal hooked nose. Stroking his greatly shortened nose, he timidly and nervously peered into the mirror which his disciple held out to him.

The nose, which previously had dangled below his chin, had miraculously dwindled, and, not protruding below his upper lip, was barely a relic of what it had once been. The red blotches which bespeckled it were probably only bruises caused by the trampling.

"No one will laugh at me any more," the priest thought to himself. He saw in the mirror that the face reflected there was looking into the face outside the mirror, blinking its eyes in satisfaction.

But all day long he was uneasy and feared that his nose might grow long; so whenever he had the chance, whether in chanting sutras or in eating meals, he stealthily touched his nose. However, he found his nose installed in good shape above his upper lip, without straying beyond his lower lip.

Early in the morning, at the moment of waking,

he stroked the tip of his nose, and he found that it was still as short as ever. After a gap of many years he at that moment recognized the same relief he had felt when he had completed the austerities required for his transcription of the lengthy Lotus Sutra of his sect.

Within the course of several days, however, Zenchi had a most surprising experience. A samurai who, on business, visited the Temple of Ike-no-O, looked amused as never before, and, quite incapable of uttering a word, he could but stare fixedly at the priest's nose. This was not all. The page who once had dropped Zenchi's nose into the bowl of gruel happened to pass by Zenchi in the lecture hall; at first, resisting his impulse to laugh, casting down his eyes, he could not for long withhold his burst of laughter. The sextons under Zenchi's supervision would listen respectfully while seated face to face with their master, but on more than one occasion they fell to chuckling as soon as he turned his back.

Zenchi at first attributed the laughter of his page and the sextons to the marked change in his features, but by and by, with his head cocked on one side, interrupting the sutra he was chanting, he would mutter to himself: "The change alone does not give a plausible explanation for their laughter.—Zenchi Naigu! their laughter is now different from what it was when your nose was long. If you could say that the unfamiliar nose looks more ridiculous than the familiar one, that would once and for all settle the matter. But there must be some other reason behind it; they didn't laugh heartily or irresistibly as before."

The poor amiable priest on such occasions would look up at Fugen,[6] Goddess of Wisdom, pictured on the scroll hanging close beside him, and calling to mind the long nose he had wielded until four or five days previously, he would lapse into melancholy "like one sunken low recalleth his glory of by-gone days." But it was to be regretted that he was deficient in judgment sufficient to find a solution to this quandary.

Man is possessed of two contradictory sentiments. Everyone will sympathize with another's misfortune. But when the other manages to pull through his misfortune, he not only thinks it safe to laugh at him to his face but also comes even to regard him with envy. In extreme cases some may feel like casting him into his former misfortune again and may even harbor some enmity, if negative, toward him.

Zenchi was at a loss to know what precisely made him forlorn, but his unhappiness was caused by nothing more than the wayward caprices of those

[6] Fugen—abbreviation of Fugen Bosatsu, who, on a white elephant, sits at Buddha's side and through mercy redeems people.

surrounding him,—the priests and laymen of Ike-no-O.

Day after day, Zenchi becoming more and more unhappy and vexed, would not open his mouth without speaking sharply to someone, and was ever out-of-sorts until even the disciple who had administered to him the effective remedy began to backbite him, saying, "The master will be punished for his sins."

What especially enraged Zenchi was the mischief played on him by the page. One day hearing a dog yelping wildly, he casually looked outside and found the page, with a stick about two feet long in his hand, chasing a lean and shaggy dog, and shouting: "Watch out there for your *nose!* Watch out or I'll hit your *nose.*" Snatching the wooden stick from the page's hand, the priest struck him sharply across the face; it was the very stick which had been used to hold up Zenchi's nose.

Finally Zenchi came to feel sorry and even resentful for having had his long nose shortened.

One night after sunset it happened that the wind seeming to have arisen suddenly, the noisy tinkling of the pagoda wind-bells [7] came to his cell. The cold, moreover, had so noticeably increased

[7] Wind-bells—are little bells hung under the four corners of the eaves, as for instance, on a pagoda. The Japanese hang them on their houses, calling them *furin*. They say it induces them to feel cool in summer.

in severity that Zenchi could not go to sleep, try as he might; tossing and turning in his bed he became aware of an itching in his nose. Putting his hand to his nose he felt that it had become swollen as if with dropsy; it seemed feverish, too.

"It was so drastically shortened that I might have caught some disease," he muttered to himself, caressing his nose as reverently as he would if he were holding the offerings of incense and flowers to be dedicated at the altar.

On the following morning Zenchi as usual awoke early, and he noticed that the garden was as bright as if it were carpeted with gold, because in the garden the gingko trees and horse-chestnuts had overnight shed all their leaves; and the crest of the pagoda must have been encrusted with frost, for the nine copper rings of the spire were brightly shining in the still faint glimmer of the rising sun. Sitting on the verandah, the shutters already opened, he drew a deep breath, and at that same moment a certain feeling, the nature of which he had all but forgotten, came back to him.

Instinctively he put his hand to his nose, and what he touched was not the short nose that had been his the night before, but the former long nose that had dangled five or six inches over his lips; in one night, he found, his nose had grown as long as it had been previously, and this, for some reason, made him feel refreshed and as happy as he had felt in the first moments when his nose had been shortened.

"Nobody will laugh at me any more," he whispered to himself.

His long nose dangled in the autumn breeze of early morning.

THE TANGERINES

ONE cloudy winter evening I sat in the corner of a second-class car of the Tokyo-Yokosuka train and waited for the starting whistle. In the car there was, surprisingly, no passenger but myself. Looking out on the platform, strangely enough there was not a single person who had come to bid someone good-bye. The only sound was that of a puppy whining sadly from time to time. All of these things seemed wholly suited to my mood. Fatigue and ennui enshrouded me with their dull and heavy shadows, like a gray and shadowy sky. With both hands deep in my pockets, I didn't even feel like taking the evening paper out of my pocket.

After a while I heard the starting whistle. Feeling tired but comfortable, my head leaning against the window frame, I waited for the station to begin moving backward, away from me. Just then I heard the sharp clatter of *geta* and the sharp voice of the guard. The door of my second-class coach clattered open and a girl about thirteen rushed in. At the same time the train, with a jerk, began to move slowly forward. The pillars of the platform, passing one by one, blocked off my vision; a tank car appeared, as though misplaced, and a porter bowed over a tip. All these fell behind me as if with lingering reluctance while the smoke belched from the engine blew against my window. Feeling slightly relieved, I lit a cigarette, raised my eyes and looked at the girl who was sitting opposite me.

She was a dull-looking country girl but interesting enough to be worthy of my study. I noticed her unoiled hair dressed in a tight butterfly knot. Her chapped cheeks had a slightly disagreeable, but ruddy glow as though she had been rubbing them with her hands. In her lap, over which lay a light green muffler dangling from her neck, was a large bundle. Her coarse, cold hands, clamped tightly over the bundle, clutched a third-class ticket as though it were her last link with life itself. Her features, coarse in themselves and her clothes, lacking in taste, did not much appeal to me. She was apparently stupid as well—could not tell a second from a third-class coach.

Lighting a cigarette and partly wishing to forget her depressing presence, I casually looked at the evening paper which I had taken from my pocket and spread over my knees. Then the pale twilight which had been falling over my paper was suddenly illumined by a brilliant electric light, and the almost indecipherable letters of several columns flashed into view with unexpected distinctness. The train had just entered one of the many tunnels on the Yokosuka line.

The paper, though illumined by light, merely showed the usual pedestrian events—the peace problem, brides and bridegrooms, bribe cases, obituaries, and so on. The instant we entered the tunnel, I felt, almost as if in hallucination, that the direction of the train had been reversed, while I mechanically ran my eyes from one prosaic column to another.

In the meantime the girl was there, sitting in front of me, appearing to embody all the vulgar realities in the human shape. I was always aware of her. The train, the tunnel, the girl, the evening paper full of commonplace events—they were nothing but the symbols of an unintelligible and wearisome life. Everything was absurd. I dropped the paper I had been reading, and, leaning my head against the window frame I closed my eyes as though in another world.

Several minutes passed. Suddenly and unaccountably feeling frightened, I looked around and found that she had moved from the other side to the seat next to mine, and I saw her anxiously trying to open the window. The heavy frame would not move. Her cold, chapped cheeks grew redder than ever and her occasional snifflings were heard above the noise of the train. This was something which could at least claim a bit of my sympathy.

But I could also see that we were near the mouth of another tunnel. The mountain sides overgrown with tall grass bright in the twilight were closing in fast upon us. The girl was still intent upon opening the window which had been closed because we had to pass through tunnels. I didn't know why she wanted it open, and I felt it was merely a whim. So I sat still feeling bitter and watched her cold hands desperately struggling to lift it. Then suddenly with a terrific noise, the train rushed into the tunnel and at the same time the window opened with a crash. Through the square hole of the window, billows of air black with soot began to blanket the entire car. The smoke dashed against my face too suddenly for me to protect myself with a handkerchief, and I, who usually have difficulty in breathing, was almost choked. Her butterfly knot waving in the black streaming air, the girl showed no concern at all for me. Stretching her neck outside the window, she looked straight ahead in the direction the train was going. And my eyes were riveted upon her figure silhouetted in the smoke-dimmed electric light. Had not then the car quickly grown light again, and the refreshing smell of earth, hay and water flown in to drive off the choking smoke, I should undoubtedly have given her a sharp reprimand to make her close

[209]

the window, for I had barely stopped coughing by that time.

Now however, the train had already glided out of the tunnel and was nearing a small crossing on the outskirts of a town hemmed in between hills. Near the crossing stood a dirty cluster of straw-thatched huts and tile-roofed cottages. The white flag of the watchman languidly waved in the dusk. Just after the train had passed out of the tunnel, there appeared at this bleak crossing three ruddy-cheeked little boys, standing closely side by side.

They were all short as though compressed and stunted under the clouded sky. Their clothes were the same color as the dismal town where they lived. The minute they caught sight of the approaching train, they looked up and raised their hands, and opening their little throats like so many little birds, they yelled out their farewell at the top of their voices.

At that time the young girl who had thrust half of her body out of the train window, stretched out and waved her hands left and right. Then, as though from the heavenly skies upon the heads of the little children fell five or six tangerines dyed with the warm fiery color of sunshine, which made my heart pound and pause for some seconds.

Breathlessly I watched, for in this instant I understood everything. The girl, who was probably going out to work somewhere, threw these tangerines which she had held in her lap to her little brothers as both a surprise and a reward for coming to the crossing to wave and shout their good-byes to their big sister leaving home.

The crossing at the outskirts of this lonely town in the dusk of evening, the three little youngsters who called like little birds, and the bright tangerines which fell down over their heads—all this that came and went in the twinkling of an eye was indelibly branded upon my heart.

I felt something like life welling up within me. Deeply impressed, I turned slightly and looked at the young girl as though she were a different person. There she was already back in her own seat which she had first taken opposite mine, burying her cold cheeks in her light green muffler. She was tightly grasping her third-class ticket like a precious treasure in her cold chapped hands upon the large bundle in her lap.

It was at this moment that I completely forgot my intense fatigue and ennui, becoming oblivious to the unintelligible absurdity of my own tiresome, dull life.

THE STORY OF YONOSUKE [1]

"I HAVE something I'd like to ask you, Yonosuke."

"What is it? And why do you look so serious, my friend?"

"Well, this is a celebration day, I'd say, and you're giving a farewell party celebrating your sailing for the Isle of Women, aren't you, Yonosuke?"

"Yes."

"So I'm afraid that what I'd like to ask you will spoil the pleasure of the party and will be a little embarrassing in the presence of the courtesans."

"Then forget it."

"But I can't. I wouldn't ask it if I could."

"Then tell me."

"But there are circumstances that make it hard for me to talk about it."

"Why?"

[1] Yonosuke who may be called "a Japanese Don Juan" is the hero in *"the Koshoku Ichidai Otoko"* written by Ihara Saikaku (1624-93), one of the greatest story writers in Japanese literature. Ryunosuke Akutagawa in his "Story of Yonosuke" assays his psychological study of the nature of Yonosuke, a well-known character in Japanese literature.

"Because it won't be agreeable to either of us. But if it's all right, let me be bold enough to ask you this question."

"Well, go on, what's the question?"

"Can't you guess, Yonosuke?"

"Don't keep me in suspense. Get on with your question."

"The way you look makes it all the harder for me to bring up the subject. Well, the book [2] about you, which Saikaku has just published, says: 'He has known women since he was seven . . .' "

"Hey, wait a minute! Surely you don't intend to give me advice, do you, my friend?"

"No, I don't. You're still too young, Yonosuke. The book says: 'Up to this day, his sixtieth birthday, he has dallied with three thousand seven hundred and forty-two women . . .' "

"Oh, you're being a little hard on me."

"Well, you're said to have had to do with three [3] thousand seven hundred and forty-two women and with seven hundred and twenty-five boys. Is that true, Yonosuke?"

"Yes, it's true. True, but go as easy with me as possible."

"But I can hardly believe it. For all you say,

[2] "The book" refers to the *"Koshoku Ichidai Otoko"* mentioned in the title footnote.

[3] The first syllables of the four Japanese digits, 3, 7, 4, and 2 in combination may read: *"mi-na-shi-ni"* (all dead).

three thousand seven hundred and forty-two are quite a few."

"I see."

"Despite all the respect I have for you, I can't believe that figure, Yonosuke."

"Then reduce the number, if you wish. The courtesans are laughing, my friend."

"No matter how loudly they are laughing, I can't leave the matter as it is. Confess, or . . ."

"Do you mean to pin me down? I'd like to be excused. Why, there's nothing difficult about it. You only figure it up a little differently from the way I do."

"Do you mean to say that I've added an extra digit to my figure?"

"No."

"Then, what's the true figure? Don't keep me in suspense."

"You're being a bit prudish, aren't you, my friend?"

"It's not that I'm being prudish, but that I'm a man, too. Until you tell me how much discount is to be taken from the book's account, I won't stop asking until you make me, Yonosuke."

"You're an annoying man. Well, as a parting gift, I'll tell you how I figure it up. Hey, you girls, stop singing that song from 'Kaga' [4] for a while.

4 A province facing the Sea of Japan.

Hand me the fan with the picture of 'Sukeyoshi' [5] on it. And somebody, trim the candle wicks."

"You're putting on mighty airs. Now the company is so quiet, even the cherry-blossoms look chilly."

"Now I'll start. But I'm going to give you only one instance, mind you, that's all."

It was about thirty years ago when I went down to Edo [6] for the first time. If I remember rightly, on my way home from Yoshiwara [7] I took a ferry boat across the Sumida River with two pimps. I forget the name of the ferry. Neither do I remember where I was going. It doesn't really matter. But as I sit here talking, the memory of the trip comes slowly back to mind . . .

At any rate, it was a cloudy afternoon in the cherry blossom season, and the whole area along the course of the river presented a somewhat blurred and monotonous sight. The water fairly glistened, and the houses across the river looked as if they were in a dream. Looking back, I found the whole stretch of river bank bedaubed like a picture in water colors with the cherry blossoms half in bloom and intermixed with pines. The fluffy mass of the blossoms looked quite heavy. In this unusually

[5] Possibly the name of a "Kabuki" actor of the time.

[6] The old name of Tokyo. The capital in those days was Kyoto.

[7] From those days until about 1950 prostitution was legal in the district of "Yoshiwara" to the east of Tokyo.

warm weather, perspiration would ooze through the skin with every movement. There was not a breath of wind over the water.

There were three passengers beside the pimps and me. One of them was an ear-cleaner, who looked as if he had just escaped from the puppet-play "Kokusenya." [8] Another was a woman of twenty-seven or twenty-eight years. She was the wife of a tradesman and had her eyebrows shaved off; and the other was a sniveling apprentice who was presumably her attendant. These people all squatted down knee-to-knee in the middle of the boat. It was so small and narrow that we were extremely cramped. And probably because of overloading, the gunwales of the boat came close to dipping into the water. But the unaffable old boatman didn't mind it at all. Wearing a bamboo-blade hat, he cleverly made use of the pole, right and left. Drops from the pole sprinkled on the sleeves of the passengers from time to time. Their sullen stares did not affect him in the least. There was one in the group who paid the boatman not the slightest attention. He was too absorbed in himself. This was Kanki, the "ear-cleaner" I mentioned. He was dressed in a theatrical version of a Chinese costume. On his head he wore a feathered cap and

---

[8] *"The Battles of Kokusenya"* was a popular play by Chikamatsu Monzaemon, the greatest Japanese dramatist, whose most brilliant period was 1705 to 1725.

around his shoulders was thrown a multicolored cloth banner. As if he were "scaling the castle [9] wall to rescue a damsel fair," he took his position in the bow of the boat and immediately began to serenade the passengers with a song as strange as was his fancy costume. I am not quite sure, but I would venture to guess that the full-blown black mustache he stroked between each flowery gesture was the product of some wig-maker. From the time our boat pulled out, he sang unconcernedly. Resolutely showing his proud profile, his thin eyebrows and thick lips, he sang merrily: "At the foot of the bank of 'Sanya' [10] was a foundling abandoned." The unmelodic theme of his song began to grate on my nerves and even began to affect the pimps.

They began to snap their folding fans; finally one turned and in a depressed voice said, "This is the first time I've ever heard a Chinese folksong." The woman sitting opposite me may have heard him. After throwing a glance around at the earcleaner, she immediately looked at me and gave an amiable smile, showing her black-coated teeth. When her smiling lips showed a glimpse of her black and lustrous teeth, a shallow dimple formed. Her lips seemed to be rouged. When our eyes met, I felt as if I was struck with a kind of shame as

[9] The passage refers to "the Castle of Shishiga" described in *"The Battles of Kokusenya."*
[10] A slum area of Tokyo.

though I had been found out in the act of doing something wrong.

If I had nothing more to say, the matter would sound too abrupt. I may as well trace the start of my story back to the time when I set foot in the boat. Coming down the bank, I got into the boat, supporting myself on an unsteady pike. Just then I missed my footing, and the gunwale, tossing up water, gave a sudden lurch. At that instant a sweet perfume tickled my nose. In the boat was a young lady. This was all I noticed when I looked down at the river from the bank. I was then on my way home from the red-light district, and the presence of a woman produced no particular impression on me. But the delicate smell came as a surprise to me. The sense of surprise brought in its wake a kind of sensuous stimulus.

Mere smell as it was, it oughtn't to be disregarded.

With me, most things have to do with my sense of smell. As an example, let me tell you how I felt as a child. On my way to and from my study of calligraphy, I would often be teased by mischievous children. If I had told my master, I'd have had to rue the consequences later. So gulping down my tears, I'd go on writing in my copybook. As you grow up, you forget such lonely, helpless feelings as are felt on these occasions, or at least it becomes harder for you to recollect them. But the smell of stale ink revives these feelings in my heart. And joys and sorrows in my dear childhood enfold me once again. However, this is an irrelevant matter. I have only to tell you that the perfume of aloes suddenly drew my attention to the woman.

I noticed that she was a buxom woman and wore a black silk garment with its crimson skirt-lining showing slightly at the hem. With her Chinese striped sash and a pair of combs in her elaborate coiffure, she had a more polished charm than ordinary women. As is described in Saikaku's book, she had "a roundish face with a light pink complexion," although I am a little doubtful as to whether she had "a perfect, graceful set of features. She had some freckles visible under her paint. Her mouth and nose looked a little common. But her attractive fine-haired brow made these faults hardly noticeable. I felt as if the after-effects of the night's drink had suddenly left me, and I sat down beside her.

At that point my story begins, because my knee touched hers. I was wearing a yellowish-colored crepe garment. For underwear probably I had crimson silk. And yet I touched her knee; not her clothed knee but her bare knee. I could feel and appreciate her soft, round knee with its smooth dimple which was coated with a thin layer of fat.

Telling jokes listlessly with the pimps, I sat knee-to-knee with her, with a feeling of anticipation. Of course in the meantime the delicate perfume and Kyoto paint tickled my nose. Moreover, soon her warmth came over to my knee. Words are inadequate to describe a kind of irresistible transport I felt at that time. I could not but translate it into action. . . . Closing my eyes slightly, and enlarging my nostrils, I breathed deeply. All the rest I must leave to your imagination.

My sensuous feelings immediately aroused a conscious desire. Was she feeling the same way as I? Was she feeling the same sensuous pleasure? So, I looked up, and purposely assuming nonchalance, fixed my gaze on her face. But my feigned nonchalance was destined soon to be betrayed, because I could see an affirmative answer to my question in the relaxed muscles of her perspiring face and the slight quivering of her lips as if looking for something to suck. In addition, I could see that she knew what I felt and that she was feeling some satisfaction in knowing my feelings, too. A little embarrassed, I looked toward the pimp to conceal my confusion.

It was at this time that one of the pimps said, "This is the first time I've ever heard a Chinese folksong." It wasn't a mere accident that the lady who smiled at the ear-cleaner's folksong and I exchanged glances in spite of ourselves, with a kind of shame coming over me. At that time I considered that it was shame that I felt toward the lady, but later I realized that it was shame that I felt toward all the others. No, this was not altogether the truth of the matter. It was the shame a man feels toward all others (including the lady on that occasion). Does that not account for how I gradually made myself bold enough to respond to her?

With all my senses keen, I enjoyed her in the manner of a person who appreciates incense. This is what I do toward all women. Probably I have told you this before. I smelled and enjoyed the delicate odor emanating from the skin of the perspiring woman. And I enjoyed her clear eyes that responded to the delicate intricacy of sensation and sensibilities. I also enjoyed the delicate shades of her eyelashes slightly moving upon her fresh cheeks. I also enjoyed her charming flexing fingers joined on her lap and the full, rich, and elastic flesh on her knees and loins. If I were to continue on this theme, there would be no end. So I'll give up. Anyway, I enjoyed her body in every respect, and it's no exaggeration to say in *every respect*. I made up for the deficiency of my senses with my imagination. I even exercised my reasoning to confirm my sensations. She satisfied all of my senses—sight, hearing, smell, touch. Nay, she gave me more than sensory pleasure.

Later I heard her say, "Don't forget your things." Her words drew my attention to her white throat which I hadn't noticed before. It's needless to say that her coquettish nasal voice and her powdered throat gave me some stimulus. But I was much more impressed by the way in which she moved her knee, to communicate an enjoyable sensation, as she looked toward her apprentice. Previously I had felt her knee, but now this was not all. Anything and everything that made up her knees—the muscles and joints—gave me as sweet a sensation as though I were enjoying the flesh and seeds of a bergamot orange with the tip of my tongue. It is no exaggeration to say that it was practically as if my knees were bare of silk garments. You'd have to admit this if you knew what finally took place immediately afterwards.

By and by the boat got to the quay. As the bow bumped against the pier, the ear-cleaner was the first to jump up on the bank. At that moment, pretending that I was tripped by the lurch of the boat —such being the case, when I got in, I thought this would also seem natural—I reeled and grasped the hand of the woman on the gunwale of the boat. "Pardon me," I said to her, with my waist held by one of the pimps. What do you think I expected at that time? I had looked for a pretty strong stimulus from this contact. Probably I had anticipated that my experience with her would gain its finishing touch. But my expectations were miserably upset. Of course I felt the smooth and rather cold touch of her skin and the resistance of her soft and yet powerful muscles. But that was no more than the repetition of my experience with her. However, the same stimulus decreases in effect with its repetition, and my expectations had been too great. With lonely disappointment, I had to withdraw my hand quietly. Unless I had already appreciated and enjoyed her completely, how could I account for such disappointment? I had already known the length and breadth of her body. . . . I had to come to this conclusion.

This may also be understood by my comparing in my mind the courtesan, with whom I had familiarized myself the day before, with the lady concerned. To be sure, with one I had talked in bed all night long, while with the other I had only had a short ride in the same boat. But this difference is, after all, only skin-deep. Which gave me greater pleasure, I can hardly say. Accordingly, my attachment to them (if I had any) would be just the same. I felt as if I had heard the sound of the *samisen* with my right ear and the flowing of the waters of the Sumida River with my left. I felt as if they were both playing the same tune.

At any rate this was disillusion and nothing can make you lonelier than disillusion. I was overwhelmed with loneliness and disappointment as I saw the lady crossing the pier after the ear-cleaner, "treading softly, swinging her body back and forth" under the banks of cherry blossoms, followed by her apprentice. Of course, it wasn't that I was enamored of the woman in any way. But I'd say that she felt toward me nearly the same way as I did toward her. Because as I grasped her hand tightly in parting, she left it still and motionless in my grasp.

"What? How did the courtesan in Yoshiwara compare with her? Why, she was a little doll of a thing, quite unlike this woman."

"That's my story, briefly told, my friend. Including women like the one in question, along with those I've had more serious affairs with, you might say I've known 3,742 women in all."

"I see. That sounds plausible, Yonosuke. But . . ."

"But what?"

"You're a dangerous fellow. Women and girls shouldn't go out freely."

"Even if that's true, there's no way out."

"Then, Yonosuke, the government may possibly issue an ordinance banning men and women from sitting together."

"Yes, considering the present state of affairs, it well may. But, by the time it's out, I'll be on the Isle of Women, my friend."

"You make me jealous."

"Well, on the Isle of Women, things are much the same as here."

"Maybe, yes, if you figure up things like that, Yonosuke."

"At any rate all is transient and evanescent. Now, girls, let me hear the folksong from Kaga once again."

THE HELL SCREEN 地獄変

OTOMI'S VIRGINITY　　　　　　お富の貞操

GENKAKU - SANBO

玄鶴山房

THE STORY OF YONOSUKE　　世之介の話

THE NOSE

HEICHU, The Amorous Genius

THE SPIDER'S THREAD　　蜘蛛の糸

THE TANGERINES 蜜柑

NEZUMI-KOZO (The Japanese Robin Hood) 鼠小僧次郎吉

THE STORY OF YONOSUKE

世之介の話

OTOMI'S VIRGINITY お冨の貞操

THE SPIDER'S THREAD　　　蜘蛛の糸

GENKAKU-SANBO

玄鶴山房

A CLOD OF SOIL 一塊の土

THE HELL SCREEN　地獄変